This is Rebecca Perry's first book. She spends all her spare time reading.

She has two sisters, both younger who she is very close with.

She lives in Nottingham where she attends Nottingham Trent University, training to be a primary teacher.

To Mum!
Thank you for everything and for supporting me regardless of the path I chose.

Rebecca Perry

THE ONE WHO GOT AWAY

AUSTIN MACAULEY PUBLISHERS™
LONDON • CAMBRIDGE • NEW YORK • SHARJAH

Copyright © Rebecca Perry 2023

The right of Rebecca Perry to be identified as author of this work has been asserted by the author in accordance with sections 77 and 78 of the Copyright, Designs and Patents Act 1988.

All rights reserved. No part of this publication may be reproduced, stored in a retrieval system, or transmitted in any form or by any means, electronic, mechanical, photocopying, recording, or otherwise, without the prior permission of the publishers.

Any person who commits any unauthorised act in relation to this publication may be liable to criminal prosecution and civil claims for damages.

This is a work of fiction. Names, characters, businesses, places, events, locales, and incidents are either the products of the author's imagination or used in a fictitious manner. Any resemblance to actual persons, living or dead, or actual events is purely coincidental.

A CIP catalogue record for this title is available from the British Library.

ISBN 9781398467606 (Paperback)
ISBN 9781398467613 (ePub e-book)

www.austinmacauley.com

First Published 2023
Austin Macauley Publishers Ltd®
1 Canada Square
Canary Wharf
London
E14 5AA

Firstly, I would like to thank my publishers.

Secondly, I would like to thank my wonderful family, my mum, my step-dad, my grandparents and my sisters for being the inspiration behind these characters and future creations.

Lastly, I would like to thank my housemates for putting up with random thesaurus and spell checks and for encouraging me to write in the first place.

Table of Contents

2 Years Ago	11
Chapter 1: Present Day	13
Chapter 2	17
Chapter 3: Later on That Evening	21
Chapter 4	24
Chapter 5	31
Chapter 6	35
Chapter 7	40
Chapter 8: 13th May, 2 Years Ago	44
Chapter 9	60
Chapter 10: Present Day	63
Chapter 11: 7th March, 3 Years Ago	65
Chapter 12: 16th March	70
Chapter 13: 17th March	76
Chapter 14: 19th May	80
Chapter 15: 5th June	87

Chapter 16: 9th August	92
Chapter 17: 22nd August	97
Chapter 18	100
Chapter 19: The Next Morning	113
Chapter 20: 15th September	120
Chapter 21: 3rd November	126
Chapter 22: 13th December	129
Chapter 23: Later That Day	136
Chapter 24: 14th February	143
Chapter 25: 3rd March	146
Chapter 26: 4th March	149
Chapter 27: Later on That Day	154
Chapter 28: 20th April	158
Chapter 29: 21st May	161
Chapter 30: 22nd May	166
Chapter 31: 28th May	169
Chapter 32: 16th September	175
Chapter 33: 20th October	179
Chapter 34: 21st October	189
Chapter 35: 3rd November	193
Chapter 36: Present Day	197
Chapter 37	201
Epilogue: 4 Years Later	210

2 Years Ago

Our eyes met across the aisle. He was stacking biscuits and I was stacking the bread rolls. It was as if time had stopped forever. He was grinning at me sitting on the floor. We had been chatting, not really working but pretending to as our manager was on the prowl looking for slackers. I had said something funny to him and he had laughed, a low throat chuckle that made me turn around and look up at him. He had turned at the same time and that's when it happened. Our eyes had locked and if we hadn't of been on shift, we would have been wrapped up in each other's arms. As it was, I was holding several packets of gluten free rolls and he was holding two packets of those cheap and nasty biscuits no one ever buys. I think that it made the moment more memorable and something that sticks out amongst the same old love stories. That's the day, standing in the middle of the supermarket, that I knew he liked me as I had liked him for months.

We had been friends for a year now. You know the kind of friends where I pine after him for months, while he has no idea. That type of friends. Anyway, we hung out all the time and people thought we were a couple everywhere we went. There was even a rumour of something not quite PG rated going on by the freezers at the back of the supermarket. Not that anything ever happened. Just me drooling on the floor as I caught a glimpse of his flat, toned stomach or me nearly fainting when he took of his jacket and flexed his arms.

So, one day, I had said something funny, he had laughed and we had our magical eye locking moment when the world literally stopped turning. It was rudely interrupted when our manager came stomping round the corner as if he could sense that we weren't working. Me and Danny quickly turned back to our respective shelves and started doing our actual jobs. The demon that masquerades as a supermarket boss, stood glaring over our shoulders, checking that we weren't slacking and then marched off to torment the newbie round on aisle six.

We both turned around at the same time and laughed quietly. The earth stopping moment had passed but something still lingered in the air between us.

"I know this great walk along the river, if you want to come for a walk with me?" Danny asked nervously.

He wasn't looking at me but at the ground. I understood why he was so nervous, I felt like I had not just butterflies but a whole zoo in my stomach. This was the day I had waited for. I had to play it cool. I had to.

"I would love to go."

I blurted out before my brain could come up with something that didn't make me look like an over eager teenager.

However, he smiled in that cute way which showed of his to die for dimple.

"Great. I'll pick you up at 11 then."

And that was the start of an amazing summer which I desperately want to forget but I never will.

Chapter 1
Present Day

This was a bad idea, I thought to myself as I sat typing at the computer in the half empty university library. What on earth had possessed me to go out last night when I have a ten-page essay due tomorrow that despite what I had told my mother a few weeks ago, was no way near being finished. I picked up my coffee and drained the cup. This was my fourth coffee and if I had anymore, I was going to start bouncing around like Tigger on steroids. I got up from my chair to walk over to the bookshelf, hoping to find a magical book that would write my essay, but no such luck. I stood browsing the shelves when a group of noisy students came through the doors. No not students, I corrected myself but young and hopeful 17-year-olds who were looking round on an open day. I hated these days and the students that came with them. I remembered my own open day when I was looking forward to the parties and independence. Oh, to go back to those happy days when I wasn't stressed. I reassumed browsing and had just found a book which I thought I could squeeze a few quotes out of when someone called out my name. Looking up, expecting to see one of my flat mates or even better, one of those fabulous course mates who had finished the essay the day after they were given it so would be willing to give me a hand. However, my eyes clocked on to the handsome body, the clear blue eyes and the gorgeous dark blond hair that belonged to the deep voice and I couldn't help but gasp and nearly drop the book I was clutching. No, no, no this can't be happening, not now and certainly not dressed as I was. If I was going to see him, I would have liked to at least be in jeans with brushed hair and preferably not so hung over that I could barely string two sentences together.

"What are you doing here?" I asked slightly angry but mainly shocked.

"Is that anyway to greet an old friend?" the boy replied, cocking his eyebrow with amusement.

I gathered my wits and words.

"Sorry, you startled me. I really didn't expect to see you here. So, what brings you up here from the distant Wales?"

He raised his eyebrow at me again while he gestured to a pretty brunette in the crowd.

"My sister has an open day here. She's looking round some different places and I decided to tag along. What are you doing here?"

I mentally banged my head against the wall. If I wanted to appear calm and act as though Danny was the furthest thing from my mind, I was really blowing it. Why did I have to say that! Now it looks like I have been pining over him for a year when I haven't. OK well maybe a little bit. Not that he was going to find that out.

"Well, I'm a student here trying to complete my latest assignment," I replied holding up my book as proof.

He smiled at the book and I realised that I was showing it to him upside down. I cringed and put my arm down, resting the book back on the shelf. I giggled nervously, waiting for Danny to either go back to the campus tour or say something else. Anything to get me out of this embarrassing situation where I couldn't help but stare at his body, realising how good he still looked.

"If you want, we could go out to dinner tonight for old times' sake," Danny replied, ignoring my surely red as a fire truck face.

As he spoke, he had gradually stalked closer and closer to me, abandoning the tour and his sister. His arms reached out and his hands found themselves resting on my hips, his thumbs stroking the inch of skin between my t-shirt and jogging bottoms. I nearly gave in, remembering our whirlwind summer romance and how good it had felt to always be wrapped up in his arms, laughing and not caring about the rest of the world. Well, that was before he betrayed me. I pulled away from him before I could wrap my arms around him and never let go.

"What makes you think I would like to go to dinner with you, maybe I have plans tonight with my boyfriend?"

Taking a step back, I put my hands on my hips and tried to control the blush that I was sure was painting my cheeks.

He gave me a look as if he was reading my thoughts and smirked.

"Well, are you busy this evening or can I take you out to dinner?"

I blushed again because the truth was, I had no plans. I had been on a crappy date the week before but there's only so much of muscle flexing that a girl can take in one evening without resorting to copious drinking. And his tinder profile was nothing what so ever like him. Oh well, at least this one had shown up. My last two dates from tinder had failed to show, I presume due to their sudden death or their phones blowing up. Realising that Danny was still looking at me, waiting for an answer, I nodded.

"OK dinner sounds lovely. Where do you fancy?" I said hoping that he would pick somewhere cheap or somewhere that took unpaid student loans as payment.

"There's a secluded café next to my hotel. It looks perfect for a romantic evening."

He was doing that inching closer thing again and I had to take another step back. Going back as he advanced forwards, my back hit the book shelf behind me. I stopped but Danny kept stalking forward with a knowing look on his gorgeous features. He had me trapped and was planning to use it to make me say yes to a romantic dinner. Seeing him coming towards me, I suddenly had a flash back to him doing the same thing one evening after a particularly lovely dinner. I blushed remembering what had happened that night. He knew just what buttons he had to press to get anything he wanted out of me.

Unable to take any more steps back, I put my had on his chest.

"All right. I'll go to dinner with you but no romance. We broke up remember, when you… well when we broke up."

He looked down on me, regret flashing through his eyes so fast I would have missed it had I blinked.

He leant his mouth next to my ear and whispered, "I'll pick you up at 7."

And with that he turned to re-join the tour, turning to wink at me, his eyes holding promises of a night filled with laughter and passion.

Chapter 2

I sank down against the bookshelf and breathed out the breath I didn't realise I was holding in. Why oh why did I say to yes to dinner with him? I must be mad. Or still drunk from last night. Yes, that's it, I am quite clearly still under the influence of alcohol and therefore still making bad choices. Standing up and brushing of my trackies, I laughed out loud at my delusions. I stood staring after the group heading through the library probably on the way to view the sports centre. Danny stood at the back of the group, listening to his sister chatting away. He said something which prompted her to laugh hysterically.

I sighed. Today was really not my day. This whole run in with Danny had given me such a heavy sense of déjà vu that I nearly sat back down on the floor again. No, I told myself, I have an essay to write. I turn to stare back at him one last time and see that he is looking back toward the book case with a look that I hadn't seen in a year. I suddenly realised that he had seen me standing there like an idiot and would probably come back over here to tell me that our dinner plans were cancelled. Much to my surprise, he smiled at me, turned around and left the library.

Picking up my book where I had left it when Danny started advancing towards me, I glanced around to see if any of my fellow students had witnessed my embarrassing debacle. Fortunately, I had chosen a quiet area of the library due to having a hangover the size of a small country. There was no one around and I let my eyes glaze over, reliving the feel of this hand on my hip. There was a time when me and Danny didn't leave each other's company even before we were dating, our bodies always touching. We used to simply sit by the pool, my leg draped over his or his arm around my shoulders as we read in companionable silence.

Great, now I sound like a love sick teenager from a romance movie. I hate teenage movies where the girl can't get a grip and survive without the boy but here, I was turning into one just because Danny had stroked my hip and let his lips linger next to my cheek for a moment longer that was necessary. Hugging my book close to my chest, I stomped back to my desk to write my essay, determined to put all thoughts of Danny out of my head.

****

It's her. Ruby. Seeing her again after she left nearly killed me. I am just grateful that I didn't react as I would have liked due to about 15 strangers standing behind me, listening to the student rep drone on about the features of the library. Her face had refused to leave my mind but seeing her with her hair tied up in an adorable bun and her shoeless feet revealing odd socks made my heart skip a beat. I needed to play it cool so like the obvious fool, I called out her name. She looked around startled for a minute and then her gaze found me and it turned foul. She tried to hide it but I knew her very well despite not seeing her for a year.

I spoke to her for a few minutes and then stupidly asked her out again. I shouldn't have as we left things in a pretty bad shape, but I couldn't resist. For the whole conversation, I kept looking at her, longing to grab her in my arms and kiss her senseless. I couldn't help but inch forward and when I could rest my hand against her hip, my thumb grazing her bare stomach, I nearly lost it altogether. However, she pushed me away and stood arms on hips, eyes blazing. I used to call this her teacher pose and she used to laugh. I used to think that it was so sexy. No not used to, I still do. What I wouldn't give to grab her here and now. What I wouldn't give to hear her laugh just once more. God, I miss her laugh, the soft light one and the side-splitting laugh that made her snort. I missed making her laugh too. I just missed her. A lot.

Creeping forward, determined to get her to go out with me again, and I knew how to go about it. Over the time we were dating, we had spent every waking moment together. When her back hit the bookshelf behind her, she put her hand on my chest and I felt the warmth of it through the cotton of my t-shirt. She looked up at me with a look that always made me want to hug her close and uttered the words I didn't realise I was desperate to hear.

"Yes, I'll go to dinner with you."

I barely heard the rest of her sentence until she mentioned Wales.

I had a flash of regret but before she saw it, I leant down to her ear and whispered "I'll pick you up at 7."

Before I could ravish her behind the bookcase, I sauntered of, re-joining the tour to hear Stella say, "Don't run of again, you're my ride home."

Throwing one last look behind me, I was surprised to see Ruby still staring at me with a look of confusion and desire.

Chapter 3
Later on That Evening

I was so close to drawing red dots on my face and calling to say I had the chicken pox. Anything to get out of going to dinner with Danny. Although, the chicken pox trick hadn't worked when I was trying to get out of sports day in year seven so I doubt it would work now. I had left the library, hours later, thankfully having finished the dreaded essay, and headed back to my flat to try and get the stench of hangover of me. But now came another issue. What do I wear? I was standing in my dressing gown looking desperately at all my clothes. Do I wear a dress? A skirt? Shall I go casual in jeans and do I wear heels, boots or my comfy converse? And then there was the internal argument of nice knickers or my granny pants. Did I want to ward him of with the big pants or should I wear the nice lacy ones that Jo had given me as a gag gift for Christmas?

Groaning in frustration I called my best friends, Emily, Jo and Gina to come into my room, I had an emergency. I groaned again, this time for their benefit to let them know that I needed their help and fast.

"What can we do to help?" Emily asked.

"Do you remember me telling you about Danny?"

"The dreamboat you spent a summer doing the nasty with?" Jo replied with a wink.

"We weren't doing the nasty... all the time." I smiled dreamily, thinking of our summer together. "I saw him today."

All three girls started talking at once, imagining knight in shining armour type scenarios where he had finally come to his senses and come up from Wales to see me and profess his undying love for me. I let myself get swept up in their fantasy for a bit before stopping them to explain the real story because honestly what girl doesn't love a knight in shining armour running to sweep her of her feet and promise to ravish her forever.

"I can't believe you saw your ex in your trackies." Gina squealed after I had finished telling them.

"It doesn't matter what you are wearing when you meet your true love." Emily sighed. She's always been a romantic. I swear, she must live her life inside a Mills and Boon novel.

"Anyway, I shouldn't have said yes to dinner but he... um... persuaded me. So now I need something to wear as I have no clue." I said, rushing the last part so they wouldn't stop and ask me how I had been persuaded. I was not ready to confess I still had feelings for Danny.

"Why don't you just go as you are. I'm sure he will love whatever you are wearing," Gina suggested.

"Because Gina, I am currently not wearing anything."

"Well, I'm absolutely positive that he would love you in that way more than if you were in proper clothes." Jo winked and then giggled to herself.

I sighed deeply and Jo threatened to leave.

"No! Don't go. I really need your help. Please stay." I pleaded to the group, all of which were lounging on my bed.

"Right action stations then, Ruby."

"Might I suggest you start with underwear." Emily ventured at which we all started laughing uncontrollably.

Half an hour later I had managed to re-do my hair so that it didn't look like a complete bird's nest and chose an outfit that according to my friends was the perfect mix between 'look how stunning I am' and 'I just threw this outfit together in five minutes'. The girls left my room, wishing me luck, and Gina's crude remark of 'I want ALL the details'. I just had time to slip into my converse trainers before my phone buzzed. I looked down and saw the name I'd been longing to see appear on my phone for the last year. Smiling to myself at his message of 'I'm outside, get your beautiful butt down here now'.

"No, we are not going down that road again," I said crossly to myself.

I picked up my bag and did a final check in the mirror before walking out of my flat.

Chapter 4

I walked out of the flat, locking the door behind me. Danny was standing there in jeans that hugged his very lickable butt and a t-shirt that I remember buying for his last birthday before we got together. His hair had that 'I've just gotten out of bed' look that on many boys, looked silly and unbrushed but on him looked sexy and cute. I wanted nothing more than to run my hands through his hair but I knew, from previous experiences that we wouldn't make it to dinner. That was something I had just told myself we were going to stay away from and besides I was starving. Cramming an essay into one day is hard and I had barely stopped for lunch. In response to my internal ramblings, my stomach gave a slight growl.

Danny smirked.

"Well let's get you fed then. I know what you get like on no food."

I smiled at him. Gosh I have missed him. Tinder dates are not the same as going out with someone who truly knows you. He reached out his hand and before my brain could scream no, my hand crept forward to join his. Now this was where I belonged. My hand in his, him striding along and me trying to get a whiff of his lovely aftershave.

We walked in the crisp evening air until we reached one of my favourite cafes of all time. It was about five minutes off campus and it sold the most amazing pizzas ever. And don't get me started on the mouth-watering desserts that just made you want to eat every single one.

As if he sensed my excitement, he asked, "Have you eaten here before? I passed it on the campus tour and thought it looked cute."

He gave me a long glance before leaning down to my ear and adding, "I thought of you as soon as I saw it."

I leaned against him, letting his words flow over me and straight into my heart. There was a very small part of my brain screaming for me to take a step back but I was tired of listening to it. I was going to enjoy this evening and then come the morning, I was going to forget all about Danny and his heart-breaking ways.

Danny opened the door for me and gestured for me to walk through first. As his arm came down from holding the door open, his hand grazed the top of my butt, lingering for just a moment. Honestly, I just wanted to go back to my flat and let him have his wicked ways with me.

I shook my head. No. We were here to have a nice dinner for old times' sake and to quote myself 'absolutely no romance'. I feel that my body needs to start listening to my brain because at the moment, it was just not getting the memo.

Danny followed me into the restaurant, and started walking over to a seat, pulling me along as our hands were still entwinned.

Seeing which table, he was thinking of, I said, "That looks like a nice table. And you can see right over Clifton from here."

He smiled. "I thought you might like this table. You always did like a good view. Although I like the view opposite me," he said, winking at me as we both sat down.

I blushed again. At this rate, I was going to end up as red as a tomato all night long. Which would certainly quell any desires on Danny's end.

Picking up the menu in an attempt at distracting myself, I hid my scarlet face and pretended to look over the choices. I don't know why I bother; I know exactly what I'm getting. A meat feast pizza with sweet potato fries. It was by far my favourite dish to order out.

Danny smirked.

"Let me guess, a meat feast pizza."

"No. I'll have you know that my taste buds have change since you last saw me," I stated.

I started scanning the menu again but truth be told I really didn't want anything else but I had to choose something just to show him he didn't know me as well as he thought he did.

I sighed.

"No, you're right, of course I'm going for the pizza."

He grinned.

"I know. You always used to order it even before… well you know."

He looked back down at his menu, avoiding eye contact with me.

It was surprising to know that he still thought of our friendship before our relationship. I honestly thought he had deliberately blanked it all out when we broke up. I reached out across the table and caught his hand in mine. He glanced at our hands and then up to me, our eyes locking across the table. He seemed surprised at first that I had made this move but he squeezed my hand, understanding that I felt the same.

"Well, I remember what you always ordered," I proudly stated, giving him a wide grin.

"What is it then, oh great one?" he joked.

"You always ordered the burger with bacon, and extra fries."

He laughed.

"Yes, I did, but I only ordered extra fries so that you could eat them."

His eyes met mine again, this time filled with love and laughter.

****

I couldn't believe I was on a date with Ruby. It had been too long. And no matter what she said about no romance, this was a date in my eyes and I was damn sure of treating it like one. I should have reached out to her sooner but… no. I'm not going down that road. It's all in the past now and that's where it's going to stay. Firmly locked in a box where it can't cause me anymore pain.

She's hiding behind her menu again, trying to conceal her blush. I know that she hates it but I think it's cute. I always have thought its cute and it's one of the things I love most about her.

I grinned at her. I know what she's ordering from the many times we ate out together even before we became official. She nearly always orders a meat feast pizza. That's another thing I like about her. Her complete disregard for expected norms when eating out and just getting what will make her happy, no salad for my girl. I also know for a fact that she will definitely get a dessert but not before stating that 'she shouldn't get one'.

When I told her what she would get, she got a look of absolute defiance in her eyes. She scanned the menu as if she was going to choose something else just to spite me. However, I was pleasantly surprised when she looked back up at me to say 'Of course I'm getting the pizza,' with a sheepish look on her beautiful face.

I was lost in the moment and I very nearly broke down and begged her to take me back. No, not tonight. Tonight, I just wanted to spend time with her again, without bringing up the past.

To my shock, she reached across the table and caught my hand in hers. I looked at our hands and then her, feeling the same magnetic pull I always feel around her.

****

The waitress came over and we both ordered, sharing a small smile with each other as we said our dishes. The waitress walked away to make our drinks and I turned my body to face Danny. I wanted to ask why he had done what he did but something held me back. I wanted tonight just to be light and breezy without dragging up the past, no matter how much I wanted to.

Danny's hand was still in mine, absentmindedly stroking my knuckles with the pad of his thumb. I couldn't bring myself to pull away, so I left it resting there. It felt nice. It felt right. Like my hand belonged in his and like they were made to always go together, like two pieces of a jigsaw puzzle.

"I am glad that you came with Stella to the open day," I whispered, my eyes locked on his.

"So am I," he whispered back, eyes twinkling.

We sat there, just taking in all the little details of each other's faces until our waitress brought over our food. Just in time or my stomach would have growled again. She placed our plates down in front of us, with the chips in the middle of the table. I automatically leaned across and took one and put it in my mouth.

"Yes Ruby, you can have one of my chips!"

Danny laughed.

I swallowed my mouthful with a grin.

"Well, you said you always ordered more for me to eat. Plus, these chips are amazing."

Reaching across, I took some more chips. Danny squirted ketchup on one side of the bowl. I gave him an odd look for only covering half of the chips.

"I remembered that for some crazy reason, you don't like any kind of sauce on anything, which in my opinion just makes you a little bit of a freak," he said quietly, lifting a chip to his mouth.

"It's not crazy, tomato sauce is for kids," I retorted.

He laughed; his head thrown back.

"Oh, Ruby."

I took another chip, avoiding the nasty sauce.

He laughed again, this time keeping his eyes locked on mine. His eyes were twinkling in delight and I found myself caught up in his gaze, not wanting to be anywhere else and not wanting him to look away.

We ate and talked. We talked about everything and anything, carefully avoiding our break up. It was honestly like we were back home, laughing over a silly movie, without a care in the world.

Before I knew it, we had finished our food but I didn't want the evening to end just yet. The waitress wandered over and took our plates asking if we would like the dessert menu.

"Yes please," Danny said with no hesitation.

The waitress nodded and hurried of.

"I don't want a dessert," I said with a cocky grin on my face. "I'm on a diet."

"You always want dessert, Ruby, even though you will constantly pretend that you don't. And you are perfect the way you are."

He had caught my hand across the table again and was back to stroking my knuckles with his thumb. I sighed. He still knew me so well. Why couldn't we have made things work last November? Well, I knew why but it's easier to kid myself into a different reality.

I smiled up at him.

"Dessert sounds great. But you're not sharing mine. Last time we did, you ate most of it."

"I think you'll find; it was you that started to eat my half of the cookie but I'll let it slide."

I giggled. That was maybe slightly true. I looked down at the menu not finding anything I wanted. Then again what I wanted wasn't on the menu but sitting opposite me looking mouth-wateringly sexy.

We finally ordered dessert and stayed chatting the evening away until the waitress came over to tell us it was closing time.

Chapter 5

Danny walked me back to my flat. I had told him that he didn't have to and that it was late but he, ever the gentleman said he didn't mind. I think he just wanted a chance to kiss me tonight. Not that I was going to let that happen, of course. He still had a lot of explaining to do about what happened between us and besides, a lady never kisses on her first date. OK. Technically this wasn't our first date, and technically on our actual first date, we did a hell a lot more than kiss but I couldn't just let him back into my life or my bed for him to then leave in the morning and never call. I had to stick to my 'no romance evening' as planned. He was only going to leave in the morning. I couldn't wait another few months to see him again only repeat the same patterns, again and again.

We reached my flat door and stopped walking. Danny took this opportunity to take my other hand and pull me closer. Don't ask when he had got a hold of my hand in the first place. Things with Danny were always easy and we just slipped back into old routines.

"Thanks for a lovely night, Ruby," he whispered, pulling me out of my thoughts.

"That's OK."

We both looked at each other and I could see the desire in his eyes. We were so close that I could feel the heat radiating out of his chest. If he just ducked his head half an inch, his glorious lips would be touching mine and I don't know what I would do if that happened.

Danny started pulling back, dropping a small kiss on my check. This was worse than him kissing me. I didn't want him to go. I didn't want to let go just yet. Against my better judgement, I pulled him back and planted my lips on his. He looked surprised for a second but then his lips responded to mine in an almost urgent manner, pushing me against the wall where his whole body was pressed firmly on to mine.

"I've been waiting all day to do that to you," he said breathlessly, resting his forehead against mine, his hands holding me tight round my waist. "And you can't imagine how good it feels to be holding you in my arms again."

Instead of replying, I just kissed him again, this time, slowly, letting my lips linger over his.

"Do you want to come upstairs," I said against his lips and raising my eyebrows, added, "I've got a double bed."

His only reply was a fierce kiss before he dragged me to the door while I searched in my bag for my keys. My hands shook as I tried to put the key in the lock. Seeing my slowness, Danny took the keys out of my hand and smoothly turned the key. Grinning at each other, he pulled me inside, backing me against the wall by the stairs and giving me a kiss that left me breathless.

"Which room," Danny asked, kissing a trail down my neck and down into my chest.

"The one right at the top," I whispered, no longer caring about anything other than Danny and the way he was making me feel.

He pulled back slightly and gave me a look filled with disbelief.

"It had to be, didn't it?"

He laughed and took my hand leading me up the stairs.

Once inside the room, Danny barely glanced at the mess on the floor, the university work scattered on the desk or the dirty laundry that I really needed to wash. Instead, he started kissing me again, his mouth hot against mine. His hands were working their way under my top. My hands, of their own accord, had found his belt buckle and had started undoing it. I let go of his belt long enough for him to lift my shirt over my head and throw it down on to the floor. His shirt quickly joined mine and I couldn't help but stare down at his chiselled chest and rock-hard abs. I undid his belt and pulled it off, that too, joining the pile on the floor.

In seconds, we were both stripped of our jeans, kissing like it was the end of the world. He picked me up, wrapping my legs around his waist and walked me to the bed. The covers weren't made but I don't think either of us cared anymore. He laid he down, still kissing me.

He unclipped my bra and flung it aside. He slid his hands over my boobs, down my stomach and stopped on the waistband of my pants. Oh, how glad was I that I had taken Jo's advice and worn my good knickers and not the ones with a hole in.

Realising that he hadn't moved to take them off, I gave him a quizzical look.

"If you don't want to do this then tell me now, because the second I move my hand, I won't be able to stop," Danny said, concern and love flowing through his eyes.

"I want this, Danny. I want you."

With that, he kissed me again, ripping of my knickers and pulling of his own boxers. He grabbed a condom that he had pulled from somewhere and then I felt the familiar thrill of his dick slowly sliding into me.

I gasped.

"I'm not hurting you, am I?" Danny whispered, immediately going still.

"No, you're not. But if you don't start moving, I might cause you some pain."

Grinning at me he rocked his hips against me and took me to that magical place in the stars where it was just the two of us.

We spent the night curled up around each other in between bouts of hot monkey sex as Jo would have called it. I was just glad that Danny had stayed and not left the minute he was done. I knew that this couldn't go on but for this one night, he was mine and all was right with the world. I could deal with my problems in the morning.

Just as I was drifting of, Danny whispered, 'I'll always love you, Ruby,' into my ear. I fell asleep with a smile on my face and my hand entwined with his.

Chapter 6

I woke up the next morning as my phone rang out. I looked at the screen, seeing Gina's name come up. I answered the phone.

"Why are you ringing me when we live in the same house? And why this early?"

"Well, we have a presentation this morning which you are dangerously close to being late for."

I groaned.

"I'm so sorry. I must have overslept. And I forgot to set my alarm."

"I'm not surprised you over slept. From the kiss I saw out of the kitchen window last night, I'm surprised that you're still not at it. Wow was there passion in that kiss!"

"Is she coming in? I'm going to kill her if she doesn't," Em said from the background.

"We want details of last night!" Jo yelled through the phone. "Some of us are living in a very dry spell you know."

I laughed.

"Gina, I'll be there in 20 minutes. Tell Em not to panic."

I ended the call and got out of bed. I hated mornings. Especially early mornings. I started gathering my clothes from last night and found new clothes. There was no time for a shower so I sprayed deodorant on like a second skin. I had no doubt that Emily would indeed murder me if I didn't show up for the presentation.

Sighing, I looked back to the bed. No Danny. Where was he? We had fallen asleep, limbs entwined after bouts of wild sex. Why would he just take off at the crack of dawn without saying goodbye. I looked around me, looking for a note. He had always left me a note for me to find when he woke at 5 a.m. to go for a run. We would always see each other during the day but he had said, he liked leaving me something to make me smile.

However, there was no note. I checked my phone. Nothing. Not even a scrappy Facebook message. Oh well. I was better off without him anyway.

With a huff, I grabbed my bag, left the house and locked the door. Thankfully, we only lived a short bus ride away from campus and there was a bus coming round the corner now. I signalled the bus to stop and hopped on. As I sat looking out of the window, I tried not to linger on the way my lips were still tingling or the way my body was responding to memories of last night.

I got off the bus to find Gina, Jo and Em waiting by the bus stop.

"Here you go," Gina said, handing me a much-needed cup of coffee.

"OMG, you're a life saver."

I gulped down the liquid heaven, feeling it start to wake me up.

"It's not all about you, you know. We want to know what happened last night," Jo said, linking her arm through mine.

"Yeah." Emily chimed in. "We tried knocking on your door before we left but no answer."

I very nearly spit out my coffee.

"We had dinner, he walked me home, end of night."

Gina giggled, "Uh huh, because we are going to believe that. Spill the beans, girl."

We made our way to our lecture theatre, all three of my friends asking question after question.

In an attempt to make them forget about last night, I asked them about the upcoming presentation. This was not fooling anyone as they all just looked expectantly at me, eyebrows raised, waiting for me to speak.

"Go on then. I'm dying to know what happened," Jo said as we walked into the hall.

Thankfully, everyone was chatting so no one could overhear our conversation.

"I'm a lady. I don't kiss and tell," I said to them, folding my arms.

"Oh, so you kissed, did you?"

Emily smirked, leaning forward in case she missed anything. Jo and Gina, copied her movements and I found myself surrounded on all sides with eager and grinning faces.

"Come on, spill the deats!" squealed Gina.

"So, he picked me up, we went for dinner at that lovely café just past campus, he walked me home and then left," I said quickly, fiddling with my ring under the table.

Jo, Gina and Emily all exchanged a look and then as one, turned back to me.

"From the look on your face, that's not all that happened last night, was it?" Jo said, leaning right into my face.

I sighed. There was no point hiding it. They are like sniffer dogs on crack and would soon discover something.

"OK, so I might have kissed him a few times when he walked me home."

I smiled thinking of the memory of his lips on mine.

They gave me a probing look.

"Andwemighthaveslepttogether," I mumbled quickly under my breath.

"Ruby, speak up," Emily said.

"Fine, we slept together," I said crossing my arms, annoyed that they had managed to get it out of me.

"I knew it!" shouted Jo. "And you owe me a fiver, Gina."

Gina reluctantly handed over a £5 note faking a tearful expression.

"Wait you had money on whether or not I would sleep with Danny?" I asked the group.

They nodded, pretending to look guilty. I laughed.

"Well, you can all buy me a drink next time we go out then."

"I mean, it's not as if you spent much time sleeping, was it?" Emily said with a laugh.

Ignoring Em, I said, "I went into that date saying to myself, that I wouldn't sleep with Danny because it would be harder in the long run to say goodbye to him again. But that got shot out of the water the minute I kissed him outside of the house."

"Where is he now?" Jo asked.

"Is he waiting in your bed for more hot sex? Is that why you were late this morning? Having a quickie before lectures?" Gina said.

"Did you leave him hot and wanting and after this lecture, you are going to run back and have more hot monkey sex?" Jo asked, winking at me.

"Um… no… he left."

"What!" all three girls gasped in unison.

"He left early this morning, no note, no text, nothing. I guess he just wanted to get into my pants one last time. You know, one last bang for old times' sake."

I smiled sadly while the girls looked at me with sympathy in their eyes.

"Come on. Let's get this presentation over and done with and then go and get waffles at the waffle house. I think we all need it," Emily said.

With that, I turned my attention to the lecturer and tried to get all thoughts of Danny out of my head.

Chapter 7

It had been three days since my passion-filled night with Danny. I was trying to get him out of my head but no such luck. His touch, like always, had burned itself onto my memory and refused to leave and his presence was living rent-free in my mind.

Sighing, I picked up my pen, trying to concentrate on what the lecturer was saying to take notes. This was important and Danny kept invading my head, making me lose focus. I looked across at Jo's notebook and copied her brief notes. She saw me and pushed her notebook closer to me. Now that's what I needed in my life, someone who supported me no matter what.

It was on days like this that I was entirely grateful to my three best friends who had helped me through the last three days with ice cream, movies and letting me rant and cry.

I smiled at Jo, letting her know I was finished with her notes. She took her book back, giving me a small smile in return.

"And for next week, please read chapter 5 and 7. You may go now."

Putting my notebook and pencil case away in my bag, I stood up, waiting for my friends to do the same. We were all heading to the café on campus for lunch before our second lecture of the day. We walked out of the lecture theatre and down the small set of stairs leading into the building.

In front of us was a crowd of people, all from the lecture we had just come from. No doubt, there was probably some hot sports science boy, lounging around waiting for a lecture as I could hear the girls at the front swooning.

"He's so yummy."

Alice giggled. I rolled my eyes at Gina who smiled back. The girls on our course were always on the hunt for new meat and we liked to stay out of their way. We pushed our way through the crowd, hot food calling my name when I stopped dead in my tracks. Standing in front of me, was Danny, leaning against the side of a bike shed, his hands in his pockets, staring out across the crowd.

"Why have you stopped?" Emily asked.

She turned around, following my gaze and leaned down to whisper, "Is that him?"

I nodded, my voice deserting me. Emily jerked her head at Jo and Gina in Danny's direction. They both immediately understood.

"What do you want to do?" Jo asked quietly in my ear.

"I don't know," I replied, my eyes still looking over at Danny.

"Well, he's coming this way so you had better decide quickly," Gina whispered.

What do I say to him? What *should* I say to him? Should I turn away now a pretend like I haven't seen him? I was about to make a run for it when he called out my name.

"Ruby!" he yelled out, causing heads to turn and look at us.

I heard the whispers of the crowd, wondering how I knew the hottie who was currently stalking towards me. Gina, Jo and Emily stood firm next to me, never leaving my side. I gripped Jo's hand, squeezing hard.

"Ruby," he said again, quieter this time. "You haven't been responding to my messages."

Still feeling the heat of everyone's gaze, I pulled Danny to one side. I quickly let go of his arm, fearing that if I didn't, I would never let go.

"What are you doing here?" I asked, angry at him for just showing up and at myself for loving that he was here, looking all sexy in his tight t-shirt and butt-cupping jeans.

He smirked back at me.

"You already know why I am here. You haven't been responding to any of my messages."

"Oh yeah. Like you have left me so many, explaining your absence from my bed after our date," I said back, folding my arms across my chest.

He mirrored my stance and for a minute, his gaze was drawn to my boobs, pressed up by my folded arms. His gaze slowly climbed up to my face, his expression turning serious but his eyes retaining that cheeky sparkle.

"Actually, I have left you dozens of messages explaining my absence from your bed after our date. You are the one not responding."

I wished I had something to say. I should be able to say something like 'I got your messages but I didn't want to see them' but that would be a lie, and unfortunately, Danny knew me better than anyone else and would immediately know that I was lying. He had always been able to read me like an open book, which most of the time I was so grateful for but right now, I could do with closing my pages.

"Well just so you, through the *dozens* of messages I sent you, I said…" He trailed of, looking behind my shoulder.

I glanced behind me. Jo, Emily and Gina were standing a few feet behind us, pretending to be on their phones and discussing the lecture we had just sat through. I knew they were listening to our conversation and from the look on Danny's face, he knew it too.

"You know what, never mind. You obviously have better things to be doing."

He turned away and started walking.

Suddenly he stopped, turned and said, "Remember the beach in May."

He smiled, his lips barely turning up at the corners and strode off, leaving me standing there looking like a fish out of water.

"Well, what's so great about the beach in May? It's still too cold to go swimming," Gina said, her confusion evident on her face.

"Maybe it's a code, like 'meet me behind the bike sheds in five minutes." Jo giggled.

"You are kind of on the right lines."

I sighed, looking along the path at Danny who had put his headphones in, in an attempt to block out the world.

Chapter 8
13th May, 2 Years Ago

It was nearing my birthday and I was tearing my hair out. Turning 18 wasn't supposed to be this stressful. I was supposed to be enjoying my week off, pushing the stress of exams away until later and looking forward to spending my birthday with my family, my best friend and my boyfriend. Instead, I was pacing my room, wondering what to wear the next day when Danny was surprising me with a day out for my birthday. I had asked and asked him where we were going and he had refused to give anything away. Not even what I should wear and how we were getting there. I had even brought out all the stocks and tried to get it out of him by wearing the underwear he likes but that only ended up with us doing some nasty stuff his mum's sofa which I was only too happy that no one walked in to witness.

Did I wear the new dress I had brought with Taylor last week that showed of my cleavage? Or did I go casual in jeans and a top as if I was going to the movies? I flopped down on my clothes strewn bed in exasperation.

Ella walked in to my room.

"This came for you and Mum made me bring it up for you."

She tossed the envelope onto my stomach and walked out, putting her headphones back in. Got to love younger sisters, who constantly have their eyes glued to Netflix. I nearly called out for her to stop so I could ask her what I should wear but her response would be a grunt or a half-hearted reply of jeans. I sighed and picked up the envelope which had my name on it and nothing else. I smiled to myself as the handwriting on the front was a familiar to me as my own. It was obviously Danny's but why would he send a letter and not just text or ring me. And he had hand delivered it but I hadn't heard anyone come up the drive way.

"When did this arrive?" I yelled across the hall to Ella, hoping she would hear me through which ever lame show she was watching.

"I dunno. Maybe when you were out this morning!" she yelled back at me.

I left my room and went across the hall, kicking Ella's bedroom door open. She screeched and yelled at me to get out.

"No this is important. Did someone drop this through the door or did they ring the bell and give the letter to you or Ciara?"

"Don't ask me, I was asleep until 12. Ciara was up though," she mumbled, both headphones still attached to her ears and eyes glued to the screen.

I walked out of her room and into Ciara's bedroom, my other sister.

Me and Ciara were closer, due to being closer in age and her being less stroppy than Ella. She would give me a sensible answer, although, when I asked her what I should wear, she had shrugged and said shorts.

"Did someone drop of a letter this morning while I was out running?" I asked trying to get across to her that I didn't care either way.

"Yeah, your boyfriend dropped it round and asked me to give it to you," she said, looking up from her GCSE revision.

"And you didn't think to give it to me when I came back from my run?" I asked in disbelief.

Honestly, ask a sister to do you a favour and what do they do? This letter could contain a clue as to where Danny was taking me for my birthday.

"Do I look like your slave?" she asked, raising her eyebrows. "I'm certainly not interrupting my revision *again* to give you a love letter that Danny could have delivered half an hour later into your hands, instead of giving it to me. And why can't he just ring you like a normal person? Who even sends letters anymore?"

"Well, I think it's cute. It's probably a clue as to where he is taking me."

I smiled dreamily, clutching the letter close to my chest.

"Go and be all mushy in your own room and leave me to revise in peace."

Back in my room I sat on my bed and gently opened the envelope. I pulled out a piece of paper folded into quarters. Opening it, I held my breath. This could be anything from a clue to my birthday to a break up letter. Did I really want to find out what it was?

Of course, I did. I couldn't leave it unread; it would slowly kill me otherwise. I opened the letter and scanned its contents. Not that there was much to scan, just the words 'Ruby, you look beautiful whatever you wear so don't panic'.

Well, that didn't help on the outfit front. As nice as a compliment it was, what was I supposed to do now? I thought it might give me a hint of what to wear but it seems that nothing was going to be straight forward.

I decided to leave my dilemma until tomorrow to see if sleeping on it would bring me any fresh inspiration. I started to make the huge effort to put all my clothes away so I could at least sleep in my bed and not on a pile of clothes.

The next morning, I woke up with a start. Today was the day I was going on my birthday surprise with Danny and I still didn't know what to wear. I dragged myself into the shower, thinking, *I'll at least smell nice*. I came out, my towel wrapped around me, and then nearly dropped it. Danny was lounging on my bed, smirking at me as his eyes raked my body, still slightly damp from the shower.

"You can't be in here! Does Mum know you are here? And anyway, I thought you weren't picking me up until 11?"

He got up of the bed, came towards me and wrapped his arms round me.

"Your mum let me in and told me to wait for you to come out of the shower. And yes, I am picking you up at 11 but I wanted to see my sexy girlfriend first. Boy, am I glad I stopped by. The view is particularly good this morning."

With that, he leaned down and caught my lips with his, cutting of my reply. I reached up and wrapped my arms round his neck, my fingers catching in the hair at the base of his neck. He pulled me closer until I could feel the outline of his rock-hard abs and chest pushed against my boobs and his growing erection poking me in the stomach. I lost myself in his kisses, as I always did, wanting them to never end.

"Get a room. Or at least shut the door!" Ciara yelled as she walked down the hall.

We pulled apart, both of us breathless and grinning.

"I think I could forgive you for turning up early," I said to Danny, untangling my limbs from his. In doing so, I had completely forgotten the towel, which as I pulled away from Danny, came tumbling down to the floor to pool at my feet.

Danny looked me up and down, his eyes lighting up with passion and desire.

"I think that it was worth it" he said, arms reaching out to pull me closer again.

"As much as I want to do what you are thinking," I smirked while he pouted, "we would never get out on time and I am dying to know what you have planned for me today."

Danny sighed, bending down to pick up my towel. He wrapped it round my naked body, giving me one last kiss.

"Later then."

I very nearly pulled him back to me and said screw the surprise. But I stood strong and wrapped my towel more firmly round my body, covering everything up.

"Why are you early then, Danny?"

He gave my body one last look, desire pooling in his eyes. "Well, before I got so distracted, I come bearing gifts."

He walked back to my bed and pulled up a giant bag from the floor. How had I not noticed this before?

He handed it to me with a smile.

"Open it."

"What, now? But my birthday isn't for another three days."

"Ruby, just open it."

I grabbed the bag and peeled of the tape securing the edges down. Opening the bag, I saw a box and a card. I opened the card first and it said, 'Happy Birthday, wear me today'. I glanced at Danny but he just smiled. Pulling out the box, I tossed the bag aside. I sat down on my bed and pulled the lid of the box. Inside was a gorgeous bikini and a flowery beach style dress I remember seeing a few weeks ago but not buying.

"Oh, Danny, it's gorgeous."

I leant up and pressed my lips to his.

"I'm glad you like them," he said sitting beside me, returning the kiss. "Put them on, I'll see you at 11."

He got up and walked away, leaving me stunned and speechless.

An hour later, I was dressed in my new clothes, bikini under the dress. I had debated wearing make-up but, in the end, went without it. I wouldn't be wearing a swimming costume if we weren't going near the water. To that end, I had packed a bag with a towel, sun cream and a book. I was standing in front of the mirror when Ciara barged in.

"You look passable," she said in a bored tone, then noticing the dress said, "when did you get that dress? Mum is going to kill you if she finds out you have been buying more clothes."

"Well lucky for me, I have a fantastic boyfriend who buys me lovely clothes to go on surprise dates in," I said giving a twirl so Ciara could see what good taste Danny had.

"Are you sure he's not gay?" she asked, raising her eyebrows.

"Based on this morning, I would say definitely not gay." I giggled, ducking my head in an attempt to hide my blush from my sister.

Ciara mimed throwing up and gagging.

"Please keep your inappropriateness to yourself. I'm too young to hear about this."

She left the room, gagging all the way along the hall.

I sighed to myself, remembering this morning. I traced my lips with my finger, my lips still tingling from Danny's kisses. This was all so new to me, we were still in the honeymoon phase, having only decided to go out two months ago. Knowing what Danny was like as a boyfriend, why hadn't I made a move sooner? And so far, it hadn't ruined our friendship.

Lost in my day dream, I didn't realise Ciara was back in my room.

"If you are going to make more gagging noises, then you can leave," I said, not looking at her.

"Danny's here. I heard his car pull up on the drive."

She walked back to her room. Honestly that girl had no idea about privacy and would just wander in and out of my room whenever she wanted to. I really had to invest in a lock for my bedroom door or a really strong blockade.

I walked down stairs, hearing my mum chatting with Danny. It always made me smile how well my mum liked him. Danny was laughing at something my mum had said and she smiled back in return.

Seeing me on the bottom stair, she stopped her conversation with Danny and looked at me.

"Oh, honey, you look stunning," her face lit up as she took in my dress and then turned and winked at Danny.

Noticing the look between them I raised my eyebrows at them both.

"Mum, do you know where he is taking me?"

"Of course, I do. Who do you think he came to about the choice of clothes and which size to get? Besides, I'm your mum, I know everything."

"And with that cringy moment, Mum, we'll be heading off. I'll text you when we get to where ever we are going."

"OK. Bye, Ruby. Have fun. Stay safe."

Mum closed the front door behind us and I shook my head in defeat.

"She can be so weird sometimes," I muttered.

Danny kissed me softly on the lips.

"I know but she let me kidnap you for the day so you got to give her some credit."

"Speaking of, where are you taking me?"

"You'll have to wait and see," Danny said, opening the passenger door for me.

"And you do realise that unless you blindfold me, I will be able to guess where we are going based on road signs."

"I was going to save the blindfold for later, if you know what I mean," he whispered, winking at me.

I blushed and smiled. Danny went round to his side of the car and got in. We put our seatbelts on and we were off on my birthday surprise.

About 45 minutes later, we pulled into a carpark. Danny put the car in park and turned off the engine. He turned to look at me, his eyes scanning my face to see if I had guessed where we were heading. Despite my earlier warnings of looking where we were going, I had spent the whole journey facing Danny, watching him drive. It was a favourite thing of mine to do as it allowed me to watch his glorious lips move as he talked, or watch his leg as he changed gear. I looked around me in an attempt to guess where he had taken me but there was nothing here, just a few cars and what looked like a big shed.

Turning back to him I said, "Sorry, I've not got a clue as to where we are."

He smiled, getting out of the car and opening the boot. I also got out, grabbing my bag and going round to the boot, just in time to see Danny lift a bulging rucksack out of the boot. He locked the car, grabbed my hand and together we walked towards what looked like a big hill.

"If your idea of a fun day is to take me up that hill, then obviously you don't know me very well," I said, pouting slightly. "And besides, if you do take me on a hike, I'll just spend the entire time moaning."

"I know you very well, thank you very much. And you weren't complaining when I made you moan non-stop last weekend."

Danny chuckled, kissing me hard on the lips as if to prove his point.

We laughed together, still walking hand in hand towards the hill. As we got closer, I realised it was a sand dune, not a hill.

"Are we at the beach?" I squealed, jumping up and down, causing Danny to smile.

"It took you long enough. I thought you would have guessed by the swimsuit I brought you."

Danny laid down his huge bag and pulled out a picnic rug. I sat down while he laid out on his back next to me.

"Thank you," I said to him, leaning down to kiss him.

He kissed me back, his lips moulding under mine, soft and warm. His hand slid round my neck and his fingers tangled in my hair, holding me close. My hand crept to his shirt, wanting to touch the rock-hard abs that I knew lay underneath. This is what I loved about kissing Danny. The absolute heart gripping, knee shaking passion and the way we could just forget everything and everyone around us.

We broke apart, breathing heavily. My hand was resting on his chest and his other hand not tangled in my hair was resting on my hip, his thumb stroking my skin through the thin fabric of my dress.

"Well, that wasn't on the agenda for today."

"I'm not opposed to changing the plan if that's what its changing to," I replied, leaning in again.

Danny kissed me briefly and then pulled back.

"As great as that is and as much as I want to keep kissing you all day, I have plans. Besides, sex on the beach, gross. Sand everywhere."

He kissed me again and then sat up, removing his shirt in the process.

"I thought you had other plans for today," I said staring at his chest with uncontrolled hunger.

"Well, I can't swim in my shirt. What would I wear after?"

He grinned at me. "Are you coming in or what? The water won't be that cold."

"If it is cold, you'll have to warm me up when we come out," I replied to him before pulling off my dress.

As I put my dress down on top of my bag, I noticed Danny staring at me.

"What? Did I leave the label on this or something?"

He reached out, putting his arms around my waist and kissed me hard on the lips.

"No, it's just that you look gorgeous. Like I can't believe that you're finally mine."

Before my mind could dwell on the 'finally', I kissed him again.

"Well, you had better believe it. Come on then let's go swim before I change my mind."

Walking hand in hand, we went down to the water's edge. Danny raced in, splashing water everywhere and then proceeded to fall over, going completely under the next wave. I laughed, the cool water lapping my ankles. Danny resurfaced and seeing me still laughing, he came up to me and wrapped his hands round my waist, lifting me off the sand.

"Put me down!" I squealed, trying to hit Danny's shoulder.

"Not until you stop laughing," he said, kissing me softly on my lips.

I melted into his lips and I felt my body slide down his landing with a gentle splash in the waves. Danny pulled away and before I could react, he pulled me into the sea.

Laughing out loud, I said, "Danny, its cold, stop."

He stopped, pulling me into his arms and against his chest. He had ducked down so only his head popped up above the waves. I straddled his lap, wrapping my arms around his neck and lacing my fingers through his hair.

"I thought you wanted to swim," I said, tasting salt as I kissed his lips.

"I think I prefer this," Danny whispered, leaning in and planting his lips on mine.

We stayed entwined together, our lips locked until Danny moved his hand, causing a tidal wave to go over my head. Spluttering, I came up for air to see Danny laughing at me.

"Just consider it payback for you laughing at me falling over earlier."

He started swimming away just as I started to splash him. He turned on to his back still chuckling. I swam closer, smirking and then splashed him. We started splashing each other back and forth until I realised that I couldn't see him anymore. I frantically looked around but saw nothing but still water. Suddenly, something grabbed by legs and pulled. I screamed and tried to swim away but whatever had my legs, wasn't letting go. I was then lifted out of the water, my arms falling on muscled shoulders.

Danny spluttered and laughed.

"Don't worry, its only me."

I hit Danny on the shoulder.

"Oh my god, Danny! I thought it was a shark or something. What if I had died!"

"You know that I would have protected you if a shark had come all the way down here to the cold English sea," he said, still chuckling.

"How do I know that you wouldn't have just left me for shark bait?" I said with a smile creeping onto my face.

"I couldn't let the girl I love get eaten by a shark now, could I?"

I stared at Danny.

"You love me?"

We had hadn't said the 'L' word to each other yet. Not that I hadn't been thinking it a lot recently, I just hadn't wanted to say it out loud and scare him off.

"No, I love the other girl I've just saved from an imaginary shark attack. Yes, I love you. And I know that we have only been dating for a couple of months but I have to tell you. I love you."

I couldn't keep my eyes of Danny, half expecting him to laugh and tell me it was a joke.

He laughed nervously.

"An answer would be nice."

I kissed him hard on the lips, feeling his lips respond to mine and his arms sliding around my waist.

Pulling apart, I cupped my hands round his face and looking into his eyes I whispered, "I love you too."

He grinned and pulled me back towards him, fusing our mouths together once more.

After spending the day at the beach, including a lunch of fish and chips, more swimming and of course, more kissing, we drove home.

We were nearly at Danny's street when he turned to me and said, "Do you want to come back to mine. We could watch a movie or something. Whatever you want to do, we'll do. It's your birthday after all. And I don't want to take you home yet."

I smiled at him.

"A movie sounds great. I'll just message my mum to let her know."

After sending a quick text to my mum saying I was going to be home late, I grabbed Danny's hand and squeezed. Today had been perfect. I couldn't have asked for a better birthday celebration.

We pulled up to Danny's drive way and he parked the car. We walked up to the front door and Danny let us in.

"Hello. Anyone home. Stella? Mum, Dad?"

When silence greeted us, he turned to me.

"Well, we have an empty house what do you want to do?"

Smirking at him I whispered in his ear, "I've got a few ideas of what we can do."

Catching my train of thought, he leant in and pressed his lips to mine. I dropped my bag in the hall and wrapped my arms around his neck. He lifted me up, pushing me against the wall. I wrapped my legs around his waist, pulling him closer to me so that there wasn't an inch of space between us.

Danny broke the kiss and rested his forehead against mine.

"How about a shower and then we'll finish this in my bedroom?"

I kissed him again and smiled.

"Deal. Shot gun shower first."

I unfolded my legs from his body and let go of him.

"Sure. Use my bathroom. I'll go shower in the downstairs one."

He kissed me and then walked off towards the bathroom. I slumped against the wall, feeling weak at the knees. Boy, Danny knew how to treat a girl right. I picked up my bag and walked upstairs to the bathroom, grabbing a towel and one of his shirts on the way.

Coming out of the shower, wet hair dripping down my back, I saw Danny lounging on the bed.

"Is that my shirt?"

"Yes, and I'm keeping it and there's nothing you can do about it." I put my bag on the floor and hung my towel on Danny's door and walked over to the bed.

"Is that so? I guess I'll just have to take it off you myself," he said, leaning over and pulling me onto the bed. "But you do look cute in my clothes."

I laughed and kissed him briefly.

"I thought we were going to watch a film, not try and undress me."

"But this is way more fun," Danny whispered while his fingers grazed my legs and started pushing the shirt up, his fingers dancing along my legs, my hips, my stomach.

He kissed me, pushing the shirt up further until my boobs were free. He broke the kiss and stared greedily at my breasts.

"I love the fact that you don't sleep with a bra on."

And with that he started lavishing attention on first one boob and then the other, my back arching of the bed, thrusting my chest further into his mouth.

I pulled his shirt of his back and over his head, running my hands over his chest and back. He kissed me again and again, pushing me back down into the pillows. The rest of our clothes were quickly shed, tops and boxer briefs flung across the room, neither of us caring where they landed.

I flipped our positions and straddled his lap. I ran my hands up and down his abs, my mouth following my hands. He pulled me up and kissed me hard. I sat up breathing hard.

"Condom!" I rasped out, wanting him inside of me now.

"Yeah, top draw."

I leant across him to grab one, my boobs grazing his check. His hands clasped my waist holding me steady while his tongue swirled circles around my nipple. Retrieving the condom, I moved back and ripped the packet open. I slid it down his thick, hard shaft and positioned myself over him ready. I lowered myself down onto him and his fingers tightened around my waist as he groaned.

"God, Ruby. I've been waiting all day for this."

His hips bucked off the bed setting a quick rhythm. I moved my hips in time with his until I could feel myself tightening around his dick and him spasming inside of me.

Sensing this also, he pulled my head down to his and kissed me hard. I screamed out his name and felt my orgasm sweep through me. I collapsed on top of his chest, feeling the last of his orgasm pulse inside of me.

We lay together, both of us panting and trying to catch our breaths. I rolled off Danny and while he got up to dispose of the condom, I pulled his shirt back on and went under the duvet. Danny came back in and came under the duvet with me. He pulled me closer.

"And that was the perfect end to the perfect day," I said, kissing him softly and allowing his arms to wrap around me.

"I know. Happy Birthday, my darling."

Chapter 9

I woke up the following morning with the sun streaming through the window. I rolled over but found I couldn't get very far as there was a heavy weight across my stomach. Moving my head, I saw Danny still asleep. I smiled, the memory of yesterday and last night coming back to me. Slowly, I eased out of the bed and crept into the bathroom. I hadn't meant to stay the night and it was something I had never done before, even when we were friends but it felt so right. I tiptoed back into Danny's bedroom, picking up my knickers and creeping out. It was still early so if his family was home, they wouldn't be up. I went downstairs with the intention to put on some coffee and maybe scrounge some toast. However, walking into the kitchen, I stopped dead. Sitting round the kitchen table was Danny's parents and his sister, Stella. I smiled, and tugged Danny's shirt down, trying to cover my pants.

"Hello Ruby. Do you want some coffee?"

Danny's mum smiled at me while offering me a cup. I took it, gratefully taking a sip of the sweet nectar and trying to hide behind the cup. I was just about to make my excuses and head back upstairs and hope that the ground will swallow me whole, when Danny walked into the kitchen behind me. He kissed me quickly and poured himself a cup of coffee.

He opened his mouth to say something when Stella interjected with, "Way to go bro. We never thought we would see the day."

I glared at Danny.

"What do you mean, Stella?"

"Well, we knew you were sleeping together cos Danny came home one day all smiley and happy and he didn't need to take an extremely long, cold shower like always."

I blushed, glancing at Danny. He just smiled at me, holding my gaze.

"And on that note, we're going back upstairs now." He grabbed my hand and pulled me out of the room and upstairs. When we were safely back in his bedroom with the door shut, he turned to me looking apologetic.

"I'm so sorry. I thought they weren't getting back until later on today."

"That's OK. I should have just stayed up here but I needed coffee. I'll never be able to look at your parents the same way again."

He laughed.

"You'll have to stay here then. Forever."

He nuzzled my neck while his hands found their way under my top.

"As much as I would like that, I have to get home. My mum will be worried."

Danny sighed and started gathering my clothes.

"Oh, by the way I'm keeping this shirt. It suits me better anyway."

"OK. That just gives me an excuse to come over to your house sometime this week and try and take it back. I'll get you some shorts from Stella's room."

As he was walking out of the room, I called out to him, "That's going to be hard, I'll be wearing it all the time."

Danny came back in, carrying a pair of shorts. It was a good job that me and Stella were the same size.

"Oh, Ruby, I'm still taking it back. That just makes it more fun."

He threw the shorts at me and turned to go into the bathroom. I quickly pulled on the clothes and grabbed my bag. Danny came out of the bathroom and wrapped his arms around me.

"Do you have to go?" he asked, "you could just stay here."

Kissing him, I said, "Yes, but you will see me later on today at mine."

"OK, that I will accept."

Danny kissed me, leaving my heart fluttering and my knees shaking.

"Do you want a lift home?"

"No, its fine. I'll walk. Its only round the corner. See you later."

Chapter 10
Present Day

I sighed, looking out of the window of the café we were huddled in.

"The beach in May was when he first told me he loved me. He had taken me out for my birthday to the beach and we were in the sea, splashing around, goofing about and he drops the 'L' bomb. I was shocked."

"But did you say it back?" Gina asked.

"Yes, I did. And I meant it. And I think he did too."

"And what has that got to do with what he said just now?" Emily said, confusion clear on her face.

"I think he wants me to think of the love that we both felt then. But that was then and we have several issues to work through before I'll feel like I did back then."

"Well, you won't admit it out loud but you quite clearly still love him," said Jo.

"Why did you two break up anyway? You look like such a cute couple and we could all feel the sexual chemistry between the two of you."

Gina fanned herself with her hand.

"And he's super-hot!" Jo did a little dance in her seat. "All the girls were crowding round him earlier."

"That's only because we don't see many boys in our course so they go giddy at the sight of anyone even half decent," Emily said rolling her eyes.

"Guys, you're not helping. What am I going to do? I can't take him back not after what he did to me."

"Well, tell us what he did. Or what you did," Gina said, crossing her arms over her chest, Jo and Emily following her actions.

"I can't. It's still too painful."

I turned away from them so they wouldn't notice the tear slipping out of my eye. I brushed it away quickly before they could notice and turned back to my friends. They sensed my pain and quickly dropped the subject, jumping onto safer topics such as the presentation we did a couple of days ago and whether anyone had done the required reading for tomorrow.

Letting my friends babble, I let my mind wander back through the years, wanting to relive the happiness I felt before Danny broke my heart into thousands of irreparable pieces.

Chapter 11
7th March, 3 Years Ago

"Oh my gosh, I hate this uniform. It's too tight and the trousers fit weirdly. Why did I decide to get this job in the first place?"

Ciara sighed and went back to her phone.

"I really don't care about your ill-fitting work uniform. I just want to go back to Facebook. What time are you leaving again?"

"My shift starts at 4 so I will leave in a few minutes."

"OK, well bye," she said not looking up from her phone.

"Love you too, sis."

Mum yelled at me from the kitchen, "Aren't you leaving yet? You don't want to be late on your first day."

"Don't worry, Mum, I'm leaving now."

I took one last look at my uniform in the full-length mirror in the hall, grabbed my keys and left.

Today was my first day at our local supermarket. It wasn't on the top of the list of great places to work but I needed the money for a new car and this one paid highly. Coming up to the store, I made my way round back and pressed in the key code. The door buzzed and I pushed it open. Walking round to the manager's office, I had a good look around. Not that there was much to see, just some lockers and a small table cluttered with half eaten food and empty mugs. I knocked on the manager's door and wiped my hands on my shirt. I was so nervous. This was my first proper job and I had no clue how it was going to go. My best friend Taylor worked as a pizza delivery boy and he hated it. But at least he had a job, even if he complained that the cap messed up his hair.

The manager called me in and I sat down in the chair opposite the desk.

"So, you will be working on the shop floor, just putting stock out on the shelves. Make sure you rotate dates. Go and find Danny in the warehouse, he'll show you what to do. Any questions?"

"No questions. Thank you."

I got up and walked round to the warehouse.

"Danny," I called out.

There was no one here and just as I was about to turn around to go and find the manager, a male's voice called out from somewhere behind the cardboard boxes.

"Over here. What do you want?"

"Um hi. My name is Ruby. I'm new. The boss said that you would show me around and what to do."

"Oh, Greg, mentioned we had a newbie starting."

Danny came out from behind the boxes and my heart honestly stopped beating. He was gorgeous. His dark blond hair had just the right amount of shagginess to it and looked perfect to run my hands through. And his eyes. Oh my gosh his eyes were dreamy. A clear blue that I could happily get lost in forever. I dragged my eyes away from his lovely face and raked my gaze down his sculptured body. Now there was a uniform that didn't look weird or uncomfortable. It fitted in all the right places and stretched across what I could only imagine were delicious abs.

His fingers snapped in front of my face.

"Did you hear a word of what I just said?"

"Um no."

He sighed, a look of annoyance flicking through his gorgeous eyes.

"I said, frozen over there, fridge over there. Make sure you keep them closed when you aren't in them. Shelves are pretty self-explanatory. Just take a trolley, load it up and put them on the shelves on the shop floor. And make sure you put earlier dates towards the front."

He turned and walked away, pushing his trolley away. I grabbed one for myself and put some boxes of crisps in it and followed him out. He was stacking chocolate bars down the aisle to me, his shirt riding up, glimpsing me a look of his toned stomach. I was going to enjoy this job more than I thought I would, especially if mine and Danny's shifts lined up again.

Over the next week, me and Danny shared several evening shifts on account of us both still being in school. Each time we shared an aisle, we would chat, in that polite way that colleagues do, me trying to keep my eyes from wandering over to him too often. Danny was helping me get to know the layout of the store and keeping the manager's wrath away from me.

"He's just a grumpy sod," Danny explained to me one evening, after watching the manager stomp around the warehouse due to the delivery turning up an hour earlier than expected.

I laughed.

"It's honestly like he's got a stick up his arse," I said, trying to reign my laughter in.

Danny laughed too.

"I know."

We both continued laughing until Danny said, "I'm glad that you started working here though. It gives me someone else apart from old grumpy face over there to talk to."

I smiled at him. Was he coming on to me? Was one of my silly crushes about to pay off?

Instead of jumping to conclusions, I just said, "Yes, me too."

After that, me and Danny seemed to hit it off. Not romantically, but not through lack of trying, but as friends. Our shifts often matched and we would choose the same aisles to re-stack. I discovered that Danny was also in college, but a year older than me. He went to a different school to me though, so I had no hope of accidentally on purpose bumping into him there. We had an easy friendship that became parallel to my long-lasting relationship with my childhood best friend Taylor. We even spent time together outside the confines of the supermarket.

It was amazing. I put my feelings on hold because there was no way I was putting my heart on the line for it to be crushed. And besides, I liked being friends with Danny. It was easy and uncomplicated. I didn't have many friends at school due to Taylor. He picked fights with some people but most people didn't like him because they were all homophobic. Personally, I found nothing wrong with him being gay. We could discuss clothes and boys and he was so much less bitchy than a lot of girls in our school.

Me and Danny were good. We talked and talked about everything under the sun. Of course, apart from the one thing I wanted to blurt out to him.

Chapter 12
16th March

"What is taking so long in there? It doesn't take that long to make popcorn. What are you doing? Growing the corn, yourself?"

I sighed from the kitchen.

"If you don't stop moaning, Tay, I'll eat it all myself."

"But then there'll be none for me."

I laughed. I couldn't help it. Taylor could be such a drama queen sometimes. But then that's what drew us together in infant school. We both had a flair for being overly dramatic and that hadn't changed in the 10 years of our friendship, much to both our mother's annoyance.

Walking back into the living room, I saw Taylor lounging on my sofa, scrolling through his phone.

"Next time, you can make the popcorn if you are going to complain that much."

I squeezed myself next to him on the sofa, the bowl of popcorn resting between us.

"Nah, you're good. You know that if I work anymore than necessary, I'll break out in a rash. And besides, I put the movie on."

I started clapping sarcastically.

"Oh wow. Ladies and gentlemen. Taylor Johnson can push a button. You deserve a medal."

He slapped my arm, not looking up from his phone.

"It was actually 3 buttons."

I slapped him back and pressed play.

"Have you seen my phone? I thought I heard it buzz."

"You really are such a blind old bat," he said, still on his phone.

I looked closer.

"Hey, that's my phone."

I made to grab it out of his hands but he turned away, stretching over the arm on the sofa.

"I needed it. Felicity was talking trash about me yesterday in chemistry and the bitch has made her Instagram account private. And I knew that you had *everyone* on your friend list. I mean God only knows why because they are all idiots who need a good slap to the face."

"It's because I am nice. Unlike you." I retorted. "And besides, you added them all on to my friend list so that you could go through their accounts when you had beef with them."

He grinned at me.

"You know me too well. Oh, by the way you have a new Facebook friend suggestion. Its someone I don't know and I don't think they go to our school so who knows what they want. It's probably a creep who just wants to have sex with you or sell you drugs. He is hot though."

I laughed. I couldn't help it. Taylor thought anybody who didn't go to our school was a little better than a common beetle. He handed my phone back to me, my Facebook profile open. I glanced at the screen and seeing Danny's profile, I smiled.

"Yes, he is hot, but he is so not your type."

I clicked on the accept button and locked my phone.

"How do you know what my type is?" he asked.

"Well for starters, he goes to a different school. And I've been getting very straight vibes off him."

Taylor pounced on that like a starved lion on a deer. "WHAT! You know him? Why didn't you tell me? We are best friends. You can't leave me in the dark like that!"

He put his hand to his heart, a hurt look entering his eyes.

"Stop being so dramatic, Tay. He is just some guy from work."

"But 'just some guy from work' wouldn't be asking you to be a friend on Facebook and he wouldn't be sending you 4 messages."

My phone pinged again. Taylor smirked.

"5 now."

I glanced at my screen.

"The last one is from my sister."

Taylor shrugged.

"He has still sent you 4 messages."

I opened the messages, Taylor reading them over my shoulder.

"Have you heard of privacy?"

"There's no such thing between best friends. So, are you going to reply?"

"I'll reply later, when you are gone."

"Baby doll, I'm going to be here forever."

As if to prove the point, he stretched out, dumping his legs on top of my lap. I just laughed turning back to the movie.

"Fine. If you are not going to reply now, spill the deats. When did you meet? Is he single? Are you sure he is not gay?"

"I met him on my first day at work. We started talking and he has been showing me what to do."

"That's a bit bland. Let's get down to the nitty gritty, all the juicy details."

Taylor practically rubbed his hands together in glee.

Knowing I could never hide anything from my best friend and if I tried, he would sniff it out eventually, I started telling him about my first encounter with Danny.

After telling Taylor in detail about my first week and a half at the supermarket, I sighed.

"The problem is, Tay, he is so hot. Like 'lay me down and take me here in aisle 6, I have to have you now', kind of hot. And I think I really like him but so far, he has shown no interest in me. Apart from me being someone to chat to while working. Plus, I don't want to put my foot in anything. What if he has a girlfriend? Or bats for the other team?"

"Honey, there ain't anything wrong with the pink team. And he would be crazy not to like you back. Hell, if I was straight, I'd do you on this sofa, right here, right now. He is probably just blind or has severe brain damage. You should try and spend time with him. You know, as a friend. Obviously not taking time away from your favourite person ever, i.e., me."

He pointed to himself and flicked imaginary hair over his shoulder.

I laughed. Taylor always could cheer me up, no matter what the issue was. He had been there for me through thick and thin.

"I love you so much, Tay. What would I do without you?"

"Well for starters, you wouldn't be half as awesome and you would probably have befriended someone who wasn't nearly as handsome and funny as me."

"Nor as big headed," I mumbled, stuffing popcorn into my face.

"I heard that. And I'll have you know that my head is beautiful and fabulous."

"Whatever helps you to sleep at night."

We went back to the movie while I mulled over our conversation. Taylor was right. I was going to spend some time with him and try and get him to see me in a romantic light.

Later on, that evening, I was lying in bed, Taylor snoring at my side. He had stayed all day and then my mum had invited him for dinner. Honestly, I swear that sometimes she liked him over me. After dinner, we had gone upstairs to my room, and laid on my bed, attempting the homework we were meant to be doing during the day but had put it off. Sometime around 10 o'clock, Taylor had fallen asleep, his physics text book laying on his stomach.

I smiled down at him, moving the book so that he wouldn't damage it in his sleep. It was quite common for us to sleep at each other's houses. It was one of the perks of having such a deep connection and a time old best friend. Thankfully, we both had double beds and he kept pjs at mine and vice versa. I messaged his mum, letting her know Taylor was staying over.

I wasn't in the least but sleepy though. My brain was buzzing, full of energy. I pulled up Danny's messages from earlier. My thumb hovered over his name, knowing that as soon as I opened it, it would have a read receipt on it. I could see the last message from Danny in the preview bar.

...if you want to obviously.

I opened them, my curiosity getting the better of me.

Hey
How are you?
A bunch of us from college are going to the movies
Do you want to come with us, only if you want to obviously?

I sighed and pressed down on the keys that would change my life forever.

Sure. Sounds like fun
What time?

His reply dinged through a couple of minutes later.

Is 4 OK with you? I can pick you up in front of the supermarket.

I smiled. This was going to be good.
OK. See you then.

Chapter 13
17th March

Having sent Taylor home after deciding on an outfit for tonight, I jumped in the shower. I didn't think this was a date. Taylor had been all for the date option and insisted I wear something slutty.

"If you got the goods, darling, show them off. You wouldn't keep Freddie Mercury hidden backstage, would you?"

I managed to convince him that even if it was a date, something slutty, would look out of place in a cinema and besides, we were going with his friends from college, to which his only response had been an eye roll. We had settled on jeans and an ironic band t-shirt. Taylor had spent an hour combing through every social media he could lay his hands on, both his and mine, looking for Danny and any interesting nuggets of information.

Upon finding nothing remotely interesting, Taylor had huffed and said, "Well he must be an alien, landed on this planet to suck the souls of pretty young girls. What kind of person doesn't even post on Facebook, and doesn't have Instagram! There's not even an old, deleted myspace account."

Taylor's information finding skills could compete with those at the FBI. If something was going to be found, Taylor would find it.

"I promise that I will grill him all night long, finding out his deepest, darkest secrets," I told Taylor.

"Alright. I suppose that will have to do. But I want a full report tomorrow first thing at school."

"Sure thing, buddy."

As he left, he called out behind him, "Make sure you use protection, I'm not ready to become an uncle."

I gave him the middle finger and closed the door, still hearing his laughter echoing round the hall.

About 10 minutes before 4, I walked down to the supermarket. I went inside, picking up a few snacks and drinks. Never go to the cinema unprepared, was mine and Taylor's motto. Cinema snacks were outrageous and for the price that they were, should be at least 10 times bigger. Walking out of the shop, I noticed Danny leaning against a gorgeous red car.

"I didn't have you pegged for a red car type of guy," I said, walking over to him.

Glancing up, he smiled.

"I'll have you know that red is a very masculine colour."

"Of course, it is," I replied, sliding into the front seat.

He got into the driver's seat and as he was putting on his seat belt, noticed my handbag.

"What's with the bag? Planning on leaving the country after this?"

I chuckled and opened the bag, showing him the contents.

"It's just my movie snacks."

"Are you planning of feeding the entire cinema?"

"No, but I might share with you and your friends. If you are nice to me."

"What's wrong with buying snacks at the cinema? You know, actual snacks that you can openly take in and don't have to bring a suitcase for?"

"Movie snacks are expensive. And small."

"I bet that you don't finish that whole bag."

"Oh boy, do you make a mistake in underestimating my eating abilities. How about, I'll give you a fiver if I don't finish it?"

"OK you're on."

He smirked, probably thinking that it would be an easy win.

"And if you eat that lot, I will stack the frozen section for a week."

"Deal," I said, quite happy in the knowledge that I wouldn't be stacking the freezers.

Once the film had ended, I collected up my rubbish and put it in the bin.

"You can't bring your own snacks and then use their bins. That's criminal."

Danny followed me out.

"Let's see inside your bag then."

"You should never look inside a lady's bag."

"Based on the last hour and a half, you're no lady. I think that I have seen you eat enough food to feed an entire third world village."

I smiled. Today had been fun. All of Danny's friends had been lovely and not as Taylor thought, absolute idiots.

"Hey, Danny, we're all going to get maccies. You coming?" One of his friends yelled at him from across the lobby.

"Sure, give me a second."

Turning to me he said, "Do you want to join us? Although God knows how you could possibly contemplate eating again after that feast."

"I could eat. Some chicken nuggets wouldn't go amiss."

"Alright. But if you burst, I'm not going to be held responsible."

Laughing, I followed him and his mates out of the cinema and towards the cars, a smile engraved onto my face.

Chapter 14
19th May

"Tay, you know I can't hang out tonight. I have to take my sister to her swimming lessons."

"It's not like she going to drown if you don't go and watch. And besides, you will have your nose stuck in a book. You won't even be watching her."

"I know, but I promised my mum I would go with her because she has to shoot off half way through. She has a date tonight."

"Ohh, what is she wearing? Is it the first date?"

Taylor babbled on. Hearing the word date was enough for Taylor to forget about any current conversation and revert to his normal clothes-oriented brain.

"She's wearing her jeans and one of my tops, going for the casual but glamourous look."

"I'll let you off this time about not hanging out but tomorrow, no excuses."

Holding the phone between my shoulder and cheek, I transferred my book from my school bag to my smaller handbag.

"Can't, I'm working in the morning and then seeing Danny in the afternoon."

"Did you hear that?"

Taylor gave me no time to reply, instead barrelling ahead and answering his own question.

"That was the sound of your best friend DYING! I haven't seen you in days."

"You saw me literally an hour ago at school. And I'm not abandoning you, you're working tomorrow anyway."

Taylor's antics would never get old.

"Oh yeah. I forgot. The mind numbingness of delivering pizzas 3 nights a week must have slipped my mind."

"More likely, you never put it there to start with. We will meet up on Sunday. Neither of us are working and we can pretend to be doing homework and revising. I'll even make you food."

"You know me so well, sugar cakes. I want all the details from tomorrow alongside a plate of cookies."

"You know that you say the same thing every time I see Danny?"

"Yes, and every time, you say that you are just friends and that there will be no details to share. But one day, my sweet, there will be and I don't want to find it out second hand."

"Taylor, you insult me. You would be the first to know any kind of news. Even if it was nothing."

"That's better."

I could practically hear him doing his Cheshire Cat impression, grinning from ear to ear.

My mum yelled up the stairs for me, "Come on Ruby, let's go. We don't want to be late!"

"Coming, Mum."

Turning back to the phone I said, "OK. I'm off. I'll text you when I get home. Bye."

"Love ya."

I ended the call and trooped down stairs where my mum was checking her hair in the hall mirror.

"You look fabulous, Mum," I said kissing her cheek. Ever since my dad had run of with the neighbour, cliché I know, my mum had been devastated. She dated occasionally and sometimes she found someone nice but nothing lasting yet. I really wanted her to find someone to help her to get over my dad and help her move on with her life but you couldn't rush these things.

"Is this lipstick too bright?" she asked nervously.

"It is perfect, Mum. Goes with the top."

She smiled at me in the mirror.

"Where is that sister of yours?"

"I'm coming, I'm coming," Ella said running down the stairs, swimming bag in tow.

"Right, let's go."

Mum opened the door and ushered us outside.

She called back inside, "Bye Ciara, be good."

Ciara was in year 10 and even though I kept explaining to her that she didn't have to revise yet because her exams weren't until next year, she ignored my advice and spent every night after school revising. Got to admire her commitment though.

When we reached the pool, Mum stopped the car.

"I'm not coming in; I've got to shoot straight off."

We didn't tell Ella about the dating thing because she still thought Dad was coming back from his 'extended holiday'. We would have to tell her eventually but not yet. "See you later, Mum. Have fun."

Me and Ella stood on the pavement, waving until the car disappeared.

"Where's Mum going?"

"Mum had some jobs to do in town, but she will be back later. For now, though, I'm going to watch you swim and maybe afterwards, I'll buy you a snack from the vending machines."

"OK."

She grinned. She was like me; you could smooth over any worries with food.

"Come on then, let's go and get changed."

"Mum lets me change by myself."

"I didn't want to change you anyway, Ella. I'll wait outside the cubicle."

"Good because you still need to put my swimming cap on for me."

Having successfully put her cap on her abundance of curls, I made my way to the viewing area upstairs. I was about to sit down when I caught a glimpse of soft wavy hair and instantly recognisable blue eyes. Danny waved up to me and smiled. I waved back and sat down. He turned and walked along the poolside to some kids sitting on the side. It was only then that I clocked what he was wearing. He was a swimming instructor. I watched as the kids jumped down into the pool and started doing lengths. He walked up and down, correcting arms and speed. I quickly scanned the pool and noticed it wasn't Ella's class.

My eyes of their own accord swept back along the pool to where Danny was now standing, talking to his class. My gaze assessed his tight t-shirt and the bulging arms I now had an unrestricted view of. As my eyes fell lower, I nearly shook myself. I shouldn't be looking at him like this. We were just friends. However, his shorts stopped that thought in its tracks. His shorts were tight and clinging to his legs, showing of the toned legs and thighs.

Then I very nearly stopped breathing altogether. Presented before me was one of the best backsides I had ever seen. It rivalled even Tom Cruise. My eyes were glued to his body and I don't think the building collapsing could tear my gaze away.

Suddenly, turned around, as if sensing my eyes on him I ducked my head and opened my book. When I was sure that he hadn't seen me staring, I looked up again. Danny had moved up the pool, following his splashing kids. I sighed.

"Get a grip Ruby. He is your friend."

I went back to my book, resolving to put Danny and his delicious butt out of my mind.

A short while later, someone tapped my shoulder. I glanced up, thinking it was Ella, done with her lesson and changed. I had a tendency to lose myself in books and often wouldn't realise the time.

"Oh hi."

It wasn't Ella. It was Danny. He smiled at me. I forced my gaze to remain on his face. I didn't want him to catch me staring at his body.

"Are you stalking me now?" he says, a wide grin settling on his lips.

"Why would I want to stalk you? You're not very interesting."

"I can think of no other reason other than you are obviously a hired hit woman come to kill me because I know too much about some super-secret plot to kill Beyonce."

I slapped my head and looked distraught.

"You've guessed it. And because we are friends, I'll let you choose, will it be death by book or bag?"

He looked thoughtful for a minute, "I'll have to go bag," he said eventually.

"Why? I could kill you with a thousand paper cuts with the book. You don't know what's in the bag."

"Do you have a brick in there?"

"No."

"A knife?"

"No."

"Anything heavier than the bag of snacks I know you have in there?"

"No."

"Well then, I'd like to stick to my answer of bag please. At least then, I stand a chance of escaping."

I laughed.

"You could never escape me."

He laughed too.

"You never answered my question. What are you doing here, if it isn't to attempt to kill me with your very small bag?"

"I'm here to watch my sister's lesson. My mum was busy."

"Which group is she in?"

"That one over there," I said pointing to where I could see her cap poking out of the water.

"I see her."

Danny turned to me.

"What are you reading?"

"*Lady Chatterley's Lover*," I said holding it up for him to see.

"For school?"

I grinned sheepishly.

"No, for fun."

We sat and talked until I saw Ella leave the pool. She looked up and waved to me.

"That's my cue," I said. "I have to go and make sure she gets dressed properly. Plus, I promised her snacks afterwards. I'll see you tomorrow."

"Bye, Ruby."

I walked away. Boy, was I going to have something to share with Taylor when I next saw him?

Chapter 15
5th June

"Let's go out."

Taylor appeared at my side as I was exiting my English classroom.

"Do you deliberately run from your lessons to scare me coming out of mine?" I asked, clutching my books to my chest.

"You know it, baby doll."

He glared at someone who pushed into his side and then turned back to me.

"Well let's go out. It's Friday night and I know for a fact that we both aren't working and the only thing you have on tonight is studying."

"OK. Let's do it. We can get ready at mine but I'll have to stay at your house. Last time I went home after going out drinking with you, I vomited in the kitchen sink and woke everyone up."

"Sure. The parents are out of town anyway."

We headed out of the school grounds, Taylor planning our outfits.

"Louise is having a house party tonight. We could go there."

"Do we have to go to Louise's? She is such a cow."

He rolled his eyes.

"Tay, you only think that she is a cow because you both came in the same outfit once and it looked better on her."

Taylor looked horrified.

"It did not look better on her. Take that back."

I linked my arm through Taylor's.

"No but we can go to her house party and trash it."

"You've made me a happy man today, beautiful."

We continued walking until we found our bus, got on and claimed our seats at the back.

Taylor came over later, just as I was finishing my timed essay for English.

"Let's get the party started," he sang, coming into my room and dumping a clinking carrier bag on my bed.

"I've ordered pizza. It will be here in 20 minutes. Did you get my vodka?"

"Yes, I've got your vodka and some sourz for shots."

"We are not doing shots. Last time we did, it didn't end well for either of us. You barely made it past your garden steps and I nearly ran into a lamp post."

"Just a few shots. For courage. So that we can make it to the cow, sorry Louise's house."

"Oh, alright then. It had better be the raspberry one."

"Of course, do you take me for an absolute weirdo?"

He poured shots out into my shot glasses and we raised them in a toast.

"Here's to trashing bitch's houses!" I said and we downed them in one.

By the time the pizza came, I had done my hair and makeup, learning from past experiences that I was better to do it before I drank too much and Taylor was dressed ready to go. We inhaled the pizza, taking a few more shots as well. Then we stumbled downstairs, trying our best to look sober. Well sober enough for my mum to think that we weren't drunk and take us to Louise's house. She drove us there, did the usual 'I promise I won't drink too much, Mum' and off we went.

Taylor found the laden table and found two cleanish cups and filled them with something red.

"Here. Drink up. We have a house to trash."

I downed my drink.

"OK, but first we dance. I'm not trashing anything and then being kicked out without dancing with my favourite person in the world."

He nodded back at me and slinging his arm around my shoulders, we pushed our way through sweaty bodies until we found a piece of living room big enough for the two of us to dance together in.

****

My alarm woke me up the following morning. I groaned and smacked my phone, praying the ringing would stop. The alarm stopped itself and I laid back on my pillows. I was never drinking again. Ever. Not even if Taylor begged me as part of his dying wish. Plus, I had ended up going back to mine instead of Taylor's and as a result I had accidentally woken my mum up.

Closing my eyes, I tried to go back to sleep when my alarm went off again. This time I sat up, my head pounding and turned off the alarm. Noticing the time, I dragged myself out of bed and went for a shower. I had work in half an hour and I didn't want to be late. Showering as quickly as I dared and then putting on my horrible uniform, I grabbed a pint glass of water and downed the whole thing. Mum had obviously left it there for me before leaving for work.

I left the house and locked up. Ciara was at a friend's house and Ella wouldn't be up for hours.

I walked the short distance to the supermarket, the sun feeling like it was blinding me. I entered through the back and signed in. Seeing no one else around but knowing Danny was also on this shift, I made my way through the shop to the warehouse. Brenda, the over-smiley checkout assistant waved at me and yelled her customary hello. I could do no more than wave meekly and continue walking.

I entered the warehouse, looking for a trolley when something jumped out at me from behind the caned good section. I screamed and clutched my chest, my heart threatening to come out of my chest.

"Ha-ha. I got you. Oh, that was good. You should have seen the look on your face." Danny chortled, clutching his sides as he laughed.

"Do you think you could play your childish pranks on someone else? Preferably someone who is at least a long way from me," I whispered, sitting down on the floor behind the shelving racks. "And while you're at it, talk in a normal volume."

I thought my head would explode if anyone spoke above a whisper.

"My, my, someone's feeling a bit sore this morning."

He sat down next to me, both of us now hidden from view of anyone who walked in.

"Did someone go out drinking last night?"

"Yes, my best friend dragged me out to a house party and we made the mistake of doing shots before we left mine."

Danny laughed.

"Well, serves you right when you know you have work in the morning."

There was a twinkle to his voice as he said it. No one should be allowed to be that cheerful this early in the morning.

"I know. I know. How about you do the work and I'll sleep here for a few hours."

"Not a chance. Up you get buster."

He hauled me up and together we made our way through the food that needed to be put on the shelves.

Chapter 16
9ᵗʰ August

I got back from my run, red in the face and sweat coming out of places I didn't know could sweat and collapsed on the sofa. I had only started running because Taylor had promised that he would do it with me and because I needed to keep up with my late-night study biscuits. But when I knocked on Taylor's door his mum answered and said that he was still asleep. I had gone up to his room, smacked his shoulder and received a 'Fuck off, I'm sleeping.' I decided to leave him to it and go on a run anyway.

Breathing heavily and trying to motivate myself to get a glass of water, I thought to myself, I really needed to find a different form of torture, I mean exercise to do. Especially in this heat. I sighed and took my headphones out of my ears and pulled off my arm band which holds my phone. It was a present from my mum as a not-so-subtle hint to get fitter. Pulling out my phone, I saw many messages, all from Danny. I opened my phone and started scrolling through them.

Ruby, help me
I desperately need your help
I've entered a bet with Stella

Why! Why! Why!
Seriously answer!
This is a life-or-death situation
That's it I'm coming over

I smiled to myself. Over the last couple of months, me and Danny had become really close. Not quite matching me and Taylor, but then who could but I now couldn't imagine my life without him.

I was about to reply to his dramatic ass when the doorbell rang. Knowing it was Danny, I texted saying that the door was unlocked and that he could come in. I called out to him that I was in the living room. I glanced down at my sweaty body, realising that any hopes of Danny seeing me as something more than a friend vanished into thin air.

I pushed those thoughts from my mind and put a smile on my face just as Danny walked in. We were friends and he simply didn't feel about me the way I did about him and I didn't want to ruin our friendship over something silly.

Danny stopped in the doorway and glared at me. "Oh, I see. I have a life-or-death emergency and all you can do is lay on the sofa. It must be fun in your chilled world," he grumbled, sitting down next to me on the sofa.

I laughed; I couldn't help it. I loved it when Danny was over dramatic about the little things.

He glared at me.

"This is serious!"

"I know, I know. What did you do this time? Did you bet Stella that you can do more push ups than her again because you know from last time that you can't."

I laughed again, thinking of the funny memory.

Danny pouted.

"I think you will find that on that occasion, I let her win."

"OK. Whatever helps you sleep at night," I said, patting his knee. "What was it then?"

"Do you remember me talking about my cousin Claire. And how she is getting married this August. Well, me and Stella made a bet to see who could bring the best date to the wedding. She is bringing her athletic boyfriend, Brett, who is practically an Olympic gold medallist."

"OK, what do you want me to do about that? You have seen me playing tennis. I can't beat someone like that."

"I know. You are quite useless when it comes to sports. However, you can dance, you can talk politely to strangers about anything and of course, you can drink anyone under the table. I mean even my dad couldn't beat you when you came over for Stella's birthday."

"So just to make things clear, you want me to come with you to your cousin's wedding, make a bit of small talk and then drink everyone under the table."

"Yes. Please say you'll do it. I'll do anything you want. I'll even pay for your dress and shoes."

He knew me too well. Dangle clothes in front of me and I'll do just about anything.

"And I know that you are far prettier that, Brett."

He leant his head on my shoulder and smiled up at me, batting his eyelashes in an attempt to look cute.

"Fine, I'll go but you owe me. And you had better pay for my dress. Just count yourself lucky that I am not going on holiday this year."

"Thank you so much. You don't know what this means to me. And now that's done, you need to shower. You absolutely stink."

"I'll go have a shower. Do you have anywhere to be? Because you could stay and we could watch a film or something."

"Nope, apart from convincing you to come with me to Claire's wedding, I have a completely free day. Now hurry up and shower before you kill your remaining house plant with the smell."

****

Well, that went better than expected. I hadn't thought she would agree to the wedding. But I was losing my mind not asking her out. She didn't know the effect she had on me. Asking her to go with me to the wedding was the first step in me asking her out properly. The only trouble was, I didn't want to ruin our friendship. And that I didn't know if she liked me the way I like her. Maybe to her, we were just friends and she was only going with me as a pity thing. Every time I see her, she looks amazing. I just want to grab her and kiss her until she melts against me. And today, seeing that ass walk out of the room, clothed in skin tight lycra and hips swaying tauntingly, I nearly grabbed her and kissed her breathless. I was going to make a fool out of myself if this continued.

When Ruby came back down, showered and dressed in leggings and a shirt that hugged her amazing figure, I mentally shook myself. Let's see how the wedding goes and then take it from there. For now, we were friends and friends we were going to stay.

"What movie do you want to watch?" she asked, falling onto the sofa besides me. She was so close. If I wanted to, I could reach out and stroke her thigh, thread my hands through her silky locks and kiss her senseless.

Instead, I said, "I don't mind, you choose."

She put on a random action film and settled against me to watch it. I leant back on the sofa and settled down to watch her.

Chapter 17
22nd August

The day of the wedding had approached. Danny had taken me shopping last weekend to buy a dress and matching shoes. It was such a nice day. He picked me up at 11 and we went to the big shopping centre in town where he trailed after me, going into shop after shop, I tried on a mountain of dresses while Danny made good use of the 'boyfriend' chair. I was impressed. He didn't moan once and gave good opinions of all the dresses. Not just 'yeah that looks great' to every dress.

Eventually I had chosen a dress that would not outshine the bride but would still make everyone's head turn. Danny, true to his word, paid for the dress and subsequent shoes. I tried to pay but he simply took my card and put it in his pocket.

'You can pay for lunch,' was his only reply. I saw the shop assistant glance between us appraisingly. I wanted to laugh out loud and cry at the same time. She was obviously interested in Danny but couldn't tell if we were dating or not. Well, get in line, Sister, I was here first.

When I got home, my mum made me try on the dress and show her. I gave her a twirl and she nodded her approval.

"It suits you very well. Now take it off before you spill something down it or tear it."

Laughing, I did as she said and hung it over my wardrobe door.

The morning of the wedding, I woke up and showered. Danny was picking me up at 2 and the ceremony started at 4. I had debated wearing something else in the car to avoid destroying the dress but it was only an hour and a half so I would be fine. I did my makeup and hair, deciding to straighten it but leave it down. Clips always came out of my hair and I would end up losing them anyway when the dancing started. Next, I slipped on the dress and just as I had put my shoes on, the doorbell rang. Checking the time, I smiled. It was Danny. I couldn't wait to see him in a suit. He had brought a tie to match the colour of my dress and I knew the full effect would be earth shattering.

I walked downstairs, being careful not to trip in my heels, carrying my overnight bag. Danny was standing at the bottom, jacket on, gazing up at me. Our eyes fell on each other, assessing, liking what they saw. I was right. Danny in a suit was delicious. I mean most men could wear a suit well but on Danny it looked like it was made just for him.

I came to a stop at the bottom of the stairs.

"You scrub up nicely," I told him.

"You're not so bad yourself."

He smiled at me and taking my hand, led me outside to the car.

"Wait, I have to take a picture. You both look so cute together."

I tensed at my mum's words but Danny next to me didn't seem to notice a thing so I smiled at the camera, my arm linked through Danny's. He held open the car door for me and then walked round to his side. I did a final wave to my mum and we were off.

"You look absolutely stunning by the way, Ruby," he said, glancing briefly across at me.

"Thanks," I replied, not sure how to handle this new Danny.

"Are you ready to impress family members you'll never have to see again?"

"Hell yes, let's do this thing."

And with that, and awkwardness vanished and we became the old and familiar Danny and Ruby.

For the rest of the journey, we sang bad songs on the radio and laughed at funny road signs. But there was something there, simmering beneath the surface that was just a little bit far for me to fully grasp.

Chapter 18

We arrived at a beautiful church and I gazed at it in wonder.

"Wow, this place is amazing."

We got out of the car and arm in arm made our way to the front where an usher was giving out the order of service and showing people to their seats. Danny took an order of service and said bride when asked which side. The usher pointed to some pews and said any but the front two. We thanked him and walked inside.

I spotted Danny's mum, dad and sister, Stella, sitting with what I can only describe as a tree trunk. He had big beefy arms and a solid looking torso. Any kids later on would have to be careful when running around. If they ran into him, they would land straight in the hospital with hardly a mark on him. Attractive as he was, I definitely preferred the tight muscles and sculptured chest of Danny.

I turned to Danny to see if he had spotted his family but he was talking with one of the other guests. He looked at me and I motioned towards their pew. He thanked me and we walked down the aisle towards them.

I couldn't help but let my mind wander down a different path. What was it going to be like walking down the aisle but wearing white, everybody staring at me? My feet gliding along as Danny turned round at the altar to stare lovingly at me, our favourite song.

"Stop," I told myself. "I can't think about things like that. We were friends."

I repeated the age-old mantra and forced myself to concentrate on smiling and greeting Danny's family. We sat down and I had a good look round the church, taking in the impressively high ceilings and the artwork in the stained-glass windows.

"I'm so glad you could make it. Danny has been talking our ears of ever since you agreed to come to the wedding with him," his mum said, leaning across her husband and smiling at me. "I just didn't think this day would happen."

I shot a look at Danny, whilst saying to his mum, "I'm glad Danny invited me. The church looks beautiful by the way."

"I know. And it brings back so many happy memories. Me and Mark were married here and my parents were married here. One day I hope that my children will follow our little family tradition."

Danny's mum gave me a knowing smile. I quickly turned back to the front, trying to hide my blush. Could she read my mind and see how much I was thinking about how good Danny would look in a tux or picturing myself walking down the aisle, ready to spend the rest of my life with her perfect son.

Danny elbowed me in the side.

"The bride's about to come in. You ready to come back down to earth?"

Glancing down the aisle, I noticed one of the bridesmaids motioning to the organ player who promptly started the wedding march. We all rose and watched the stunning bride walk in on her father's arm. I turned around to look at the groom, his face lighting up as though there was no one else in the room apart from her. His eyes never left hers and you could feel the love between them. I sighed. This was what every couple should aim for in marriage.

"Why are you facing the wrong way? Aren't girls supposed to keep their eyes glued to the bride to check out her dress?" Danny whispered in my ear.

"Well, I'm not most girls. And besides, seeing the look on the groom's face is by far the best. And most telling. You can see the dress anytime you want but the groom's face as he sees his bride for the first time, now that's a rare treat."

"That's cute. I've never heard that one before."

"Every groom is different as well. You have various degrees of love, disbelief and wonder. You even have a few 'oh shit, I'm getting married' looks. But they all show their true feelings and I think that's magical."

I glanced at the bride as she passed our pew, thinking to myself, I'm so glad that we were sitting furthest away from the aisle. I turned back to Danny, seeing his eyes light up with held in laughter. I grinned at him and squeezed his hand. Don't ask me what possessed me to do that but I did so there's no taking that back. I was about to withdraw my hand from his when he squeezed mine and kept hold. We sat back down, hand in hand, facing the front ready for the ceremony to start. Neither of us noticed his mum's head peering round at us, with a look of hope on her face.

The ceremony was beautiful. Danny eventually let go of my hand when we stood up for the first song and I missed his warmth. I nearly sat on my hand in the hope of restraining myself from grabbing his hand again.

After the 'I do's', we all stood and watched the happy couple leave the church. Bridesmaids and best men followed, leaving to take hundreds of pictures outside the church. We weren't close family so we were spared the initial picture rush here, so we were going to go on to the reception.

"Hold on, we need pictures," Danny's mum said, ushering us towards the scenic rose bushes behind the church.

I smiled. Danny's mum was a stickler for pictures being taken. Every big event, you could guarantee that she would be there with the camera. It was nice though, to capture the moment to look back on for years to come.

Danny and his family gathered round and started taking pictures while me and Stella's tree trunk stood and watched. They took pictures in pairs, of everybody on their own and as groups of three.

I stepped forward.

"I'll take one of the four of you. You all look so nice."

Danny's mum smiled and handed me her phone.

"OK, dear, can you take a few please?"

I nodded and snapped a few shots.

"Mum, can you take a picture of me and Brett?"

Danny's mum nodded and took her phone back from me.

Danny came to stand by my side, whispering in my ear, "So that's what a tree trunk looks like."

I laughed, slapping my hand over my mouth when I realised that I had laughed out loud. Danny laughed alongside me until Stella shot daggers at us and we turned away.

"Well, that has brightened my day," Danny said trying to smother his laughter.

"And we're not even at the best part yet."

At Danny's look, I added, "We have the dancing and of course the food to go. The food is by far the best part of any social gathering. Especially weddings because you know, cake."

"Oh, I am so glad that I brought you with me. This would have been dull without you."

"Don't move, you look perfect together."

We both snapped our heads up, finding that during our brief exchange, we had drawn closer together, our hands brushing and our heads bent close together. We must have looked like lovers, sharing an intimate thought. Danny's mum started snapping more pictures on her phone.

"Oh, look how cute they look, Mark! Don't they just complement each other so well?"

Danny's dad just nodded gruffly, getting his car keys out of his pocket and already heading towards his car. Mark was always a bit on the quiet side, leaving Rosetta to do all the talking in their relationship but I knew that he had a heart of gold from Danny's stories.

"Mum, we really have to go. Look they are nearly finished with the professional photos and you said that you wanted to get to the reception before the bride and groom arrived so that you could photograph their entrance." Danny winked at me and pulled me towards his car. "We'll see you there."

I waved goodbye before getting into the car. Danny watched his dad reverse out of the church car park and on to the road. He got into the car himself and just sat there.

"Do you know how to drive? You just turn on the engine and press down on the gas pedal," I said, nudging his arm gently.

"I know how to drive and it's a bit more complicated than just 'pushing down the gas pedal' you know."

He air quoted the gas pedal comment, grinning at me.

"Well, what would I know? I'm only a learner. Shall we go?"

Danny sat for a moment just staring at me. I was beginning to wonder if I had mascara running down my face or something when he turned in his seat and started the engine.

"One wedding reception, here we come."

I sat back in my seat. Whatever weird moment that had happened, was now firmly over. Maybe it was just my imagination but Danny was looking at me like he needed to say something important. Not that he would have said what I wanted him to say.

"Let's go and get drunk!" I cheered.

Danny cheered alongside me and checking both ways, we pulled out of the church.

At the reception, Danny got us both a glass of champagne. He handed me my glass and we clinked them together in a silent toast.

"For the first time, Mr and Mrs Smith."

Applause went up in the room as the bride and groom entered the room. I glimpsed Danny's mum, Rosetta up front, snapping away on her phone, taking picture after picture. The bride really did look beautiful, in her full white dress and lace train. Once again, my mind wandered down that dangerous path of my own wedding to Danny and how our friends and families would be gathered to celebrate our love. I mentally shook myself. Coming to this wedding was such a bad idea, how did I let Danny talk me into doing this?

Before I knew it, the happy couple were before us, the groom shaking Danny's hand and the bride kissing Danny's cheek.

"We're so glad you could make it, Danny. I've already seen Rosetta at the front of the mob, snapping away on her phone. Honestly, we should have used her as our professional photographer."

"I apologise for my mother; she sometimes gets a bit carried away," Danny replied with a laugh.

"It's OK. She will have some stunning pictures."

Glancing past Danny, the bride noticed me.

"And who is this beautiful lady you have brought along?"

Danny turned to me as well.

"Claire, this is my date, Ruby."

"Date?"

Claire kissed my check.

"I hope you enjoy the rest of the evening."

With that she turned and walked away to greet the next family. I ran Danny's choice of words over in my mind. More specifically his choice of word, the word 'date'. What did he mean by that? Was it that the word date was typically used when talking about weddings and it was just easier or was it meant as a boyfriend/girlfriend thing and we were on a proper date? Did Danny have feelings for me? What was I going to do? Questions kept swirling round in my head and I knew I needed answers.

"Danny," I said, squeezing his arm where my hand was resting, "what did you mean when you introduced me as your date?"

Danny busied himself scanning the drinks menu at the bar.

"Um, you know, it's just easier than explaining that we are friends but you are here as my almost 'fake date'."

He air quoted at this last bit, still looking at the menu.

"Yeah OK. Don't want to confuse anybody, do we?"

I laughed nervously.

Danny finally looked at me, his expression blank. He turned back to the bar, asking the bartender for some more champagne and a vodka and lemonade.

"Let's get this party started."

Danny's meaning was clear. He didn't think of this as a date and he certainly didn't think of me as anything more than a friend. I gratefully took my drinks from Danny, downing the vodka. The buzz settled in from the drink, helping me to forget my feelings and the disappointment I felt at Danny's words.

"Yes let's," I said to Danny, slamming my empty glass down onto the bar top.

He smirked.

"Let's go put that vodka into good use. We're sitting at the same table as Stella and her body builder."

"Lead the way then, good sir."

Danny mocked a bow at me and then pulling my arm through his, we made our way through the tables and took a seat, just in time for the meal to be brought through.

After the meal, which was heavenly, we sat back for the speeches. Danny and I had drunk a considerable amount of the free provided wine on the table and we were pleasantly squiffy. Waiters had come around giving flutes of champagne to everyone ready for the toasts and I was eyeing up Danny's unfinished dessert.

"Go on take it," he said, noticing my not so subtle looks at his plate. "I know you want to eat it."

"I don't know what you mean, Danny."

I smiled innocently at him.

"Ruby, I think that everyone on this table can see the desire in your eyes whenever you look at my plate. Which by the way is always," he said nudging his plate closer to me.

I glanced longingly at the gorgeous cheesecake, and then back to my own empty plate. I had wolfed down my slice, the creamy cheesecake practically melting in my mouth and the sharp raspberries giving it that wonderful tangy flavour that stayed in my mouth.

"I mean, only if you don't want it."

Danny shook his head.

"Well in that case it would be rude not to. Very selfish of me to refuse. And if you think about it then I am really helping not only my friend but the environment as well, cutting down on food waste."

As I spoke, I already had my fork in hand, spearing some of the delicious dessert.

"Whatever helps you to sleep at night," Danny said, pushing the plate more firmly in front of me.

"Oh, my goodness, this is heavenly."

"Shall I give the two of you a minute or would you prefer to get a room?" Danny muttered dryly.

"Yeah, actually a room would be great. I would obviously need more of this cheesecake. Can you imagine, a whole room with just this in? Honestly, I would marry this cheesecake if I could."

"I don't think that it is completely legal in this country but try somewhere weird where they let you marry your desserts. Oh sorry, your *friend's* desserts."

"That's not my fault if you couldn't finish a very small slice of cheesecake," I replied, shoving more into my mouth.

"Well, we don't all have endless pits in place of our stomachs."

I laughed.

"It is one of my many skills."

Danny laughed too and almost too quietly to hear whispered, "Yes one of many, many talents."

I was about to ask him to repeat himself, when the head waiter tapped a glass, calling for quiet as the groom stood up to make his speech. The room fell silent and the groom started talking, holding his bride's hand and his eyes never leaving hers.

"Drink if he says 'love'," Danny whispered in my ear.

"OK and drink if he mentions any innuendoes," I replied.

Stella overheard us and added her own.

"Also drink if anyone mentions a how-we-met-story."

Danny smirked at her.

"OK you're on."

We turned back to the speeches, just in time for the groom to say, "And I remember when I first saw Claire…"

We all glanced at one another and took a swig of our drinks.

By the end of the speeches, I had a nice buzz going. I was at a good stage of being drunk enough to start dancing but not yet drunk enough to start wobbling. Stella's boyfriend, Brett had also joined our drinking game, each off us adding a few more things to raise our glasses to. Someone announced the bride and groom's first dance and we all turned to watch.

I loved weddings. The romance, the celebration, the food, the company. I glanced at Danny, his eyes dancing in the dim light of the room. His gaze was locked on his cousin, dancing away with her husband so I had an unrestricted view of him. I liked these moments when I could watch Danny without him thinking I was a complete nutter.

Danny turned towards me, taking me off guard for a minute. I grabbed my drink and took a long sip to calm my nerves.

"Shall we dance?" Danny asked, offering his hand.

I smiled, glad to be given a chance to be held in his arms or even just dance near him. Luckily for me, the DJ was still on a slow song. I accepted his hand and we made our way over to the dance floor, joining other couples, including Danny's parents and sister.

Danny placed his hands on my waist and I put my hands round his neck. We smiled at each other, swaying slightly back and forth. Behind me I heard Stella wince in pain as Brett stepped on her foot for the second time.

Me and Danny caught each other's eyes and laughed silently. Brett may be a big, muscled man but it looked like he had two left feet. Danny twirled us around, his hands feeling right on my waist as if they were made to be there.

The slow song came to an end all too soon and the DJ started playing wedding favourites. Danny pulled me closer, whispering in my ear, "Let's show them what we can do."

At that we pulled apart and started dancing. I lost myself in the music, as I always did. I loved dancing, just letting my body move to the music. But especially now, with Danny so close to me, our hands always touching or arms brushing against each other. We danced and danced, me letting my worries slip away and Danny, I presume, feeling smug that he had won his sister's bet. I glanced across at our table to find Brett sitting down and Stella dancing just behind us.

I stopped dancing and pulled Danny away from the dance floor.

"I need a drink and some air," I said to him.

He nodded and we went off to the bar.

"Two vodka lemonades please," Danny said to the barman.

I went to retrieve my purse to pay for them but Danny shook his head.

"Dad's paying for all our drinks. Big bonus at work."

Taking my glass, I raised it to Danny.

"Well cheers to your dad's job then."

We clinked glasses.

"Shall we go outside?"

****

Ruby slid her arm through mine. I loved the feel of her hand round my arm. We walked outside, letting the cool air rush over us. Ruby's cheeks were flushed red from the alcohol and the dancing and I couldn't help but stare. Even in a flushed state, she was perfect. And she didn't even realise it. I sighed to myself.

Asking her to the wedding was so that I could man up and ask her out properly. However, when the perfect opening came up, I froze. I cursed my casual use of the word 'date' to my cousin earlier and then cursed my explanation. It was clear from the expression on her face though, that she didn't think this was a date and that she didn't want this to be a date. Her voice had been panicky, her eyes wide with shock. I could never ask her out, not when it was clear she didn't want that.

I glanced down at her. The dress she had chosen was a deep red, sitting just above her knee. My favourite part of her dress though was definitely the plunging neck line which I found myself staring at quite frequently. I was sure my family had noticed my lack of focus on the wedding and speeches but I didn't care. It was magnetic, my eyes being drawn to her chest as if they had a mind of their own.

Shaking myself, I turned back to the night sky. The stars had come out and I felt like we were in our own little oasis, no one else in sight. This was the perfect time to ask Ruby to come out on a date with me. I downed the rest of my drink; call it liquid courage and I was about to open my mouth to ask her when she interrupted me first.

"Oh, I love this song! Let's go."

She grabbed my hand and pulled me inside. I followed, helplessly. I would honestly do anything for this wonderful girl in front of me. For now, I guess I would have to be content with holding her close and letting my imagination run away with me, imagining kissing her and never stopping.

Chapter 19
The Next Morning

I woke up, my head pounding and my eyes screwed shut against the bright light coming into the room. Sitting up, I managed to glance around. This wasn't my bedroom. Where was I? I remember drinking last night. Maybe me and Taylor had gone out and I had managed to go home with someone else. As my eyes took in the scene before me, I noticed another bed next to mine with the handsomely familiar figure of Danny sprawled out and snoring away.

It all came back to me. Danny's cousin's wedding. The drinking. The dancing. The thoughts of kissing Danny outside under the stars.

I stumbled out of bed, going into the bathroom to get a drink of water and an aspirin. Gulping down the water, I headed back into the bedroom to find Danny awake and looking just as dreadful as I felt. I held out the water and another aspirin for him which he took from me as though I was offering eternal youth or the cure for cancer. He too gulped down the rest of my drink and tablet.

"So how did I do last night?" I asked, sitting cautiously down next to Danny on the bed.

He smiled at me.

"Wonderfully. Stella won't know what hit her. Brett was no match for you."

Danny pulled the duvet back over his legs and mine.

"We have the room until tomorrow morning. Mum thought it would be better this way so we could all sleep off our hangovers before driving. So, we could see if there are any movies on the TV and order a giant pizza."

"Sounds good. And we all know that greasy pizza is the best hangover cure possible. I'm going to go and shower while you order the pizza. I'll have…"

"A meat feast, large, with a side of pizza rolls. Yeah, yeah, I know. Go and have your shower."

"Um thanks. There's cash in my purse."

Danny helps his hand to his heart.

"Ruby, I'm not some paid evening entertainment. And even if I was, you wouldn't be able to afford my services."

Throwing my head back and laughing I said, "Don't flatter yourself. It's for the pizza."

Still chuckling, I stripped off yesterday's dress, got into the warm shower and I thought over our brief exchange. It was days like this that made me fall for Danny more and more. I liked that we could go from silly to serious to flirty all without anything being ruined. I only wish that the flirting could progress to actual kissing and dating.

Sighing, I got out of the shower and wrapped a towel round my body as I thought of last night. After the fifth vodka, my memories started going a little hazy but I could remember clearly the dinner, stealing Danny's dessert, the speeches and the dancing. And the short walk under the stars in which I wished with all my heart that Danny would have grabbed me, pushed me against the tree and had his way with me.

Taylor would say that I needed to take the bull by the horns and just ask Danny out. Or kiss him. But however easy that would be for Taylor, I just wasn't confident enough. What if I ruined our friendship and he didn't return the feelings? Danny had only been in my life for a few months but I already couldn't imagine him leaving it.

"Pizza is going to be here in five minutes. Are you done in there?"

"Yeah, give me two minutes," I replied, rubbing myself dry and pulling on my comfortable sweats and hoodie.

I came out of the bathroom and Danny went in for a quick shower. Last night, or rather early this morning, we had both collapsed on to our beds and fallen asleep straight away, neither of us bothering to even take of shoes or clothes, let alone shower.

I plopped onto Danny's bed as it was the one facing the TV and started flicking through the channels until I settled on a channel with a movie about to start.

Danny came back in to the room, his towel hanging dangerously low on his hips and his chest still slightly damp from the shower.

"I forgot my clothes," he mumbled, grabbing some from his bag and shuffling back to the bathroom. I couldn't keep my eyes away. His muscled chest and nice abs. And that towel! I fanned myself, thinking it wouldn't take much for that towel to slip to much more appealing sights. I just wanted to run my hands and then my tongue over the droplets escaping down his chest.

I was still in my slightly pornographic daydream when Danny came back into the room and looked at me weirdly.

"Did you choose a movie?" he asked, rubbing the towel through his hair.

"Um yeah. It's an old one but there's nothing else on."

He glanced at the screen and seeing the movie, smiled. I knew Danny loved any action film, especially ones with fast cars. He sat down next to me on the bed just as the hotel phone rang.

I answered.

"Hello. OK. Thank you. I'll be right down."

Putting the phone back down, I said to Danny, "That's the pizza."

Danny started to get off the bed but I pushed his shoulder down, stopping him.

"I'll get it."

He started protesting but I was already up and going out of the door.

"Ruby, you need shoes on!" Danny yelled after me.

"No, I don't, I'm not going outside."

I heard Danny chuckling as I went down the hall. Me not wearing shoes had always caused Danny to laugh. He thought it was hysterical that I went everywhere without shoes. Or just took them off at random times. I went downstairs, the pizza guy standing in the hotel lobby. Paying him, I took the pizza from him and lifted the lid. The greasy, meaty smell greeted me, making my mouth water. I could feel the smell alone starting to cure my hangover.

Before I ate the whole pizza there and then, I trudged upstairs back to my room. I came back in and placed the pizza on the bed, sitting down next to Danny.

"Bon appetit," I said, grabbing a slice.

We sat in companionable silence, eating pizza and watching the movie. We had the sound on low to avoid adding to our hangovers. Every now and then, I would glance across to Danny, his eyes glued to the TV screen, so I could take in all the little details of his face. Creepy I know but I couldn't help myself. He was just so damn perfect.

Returning my gaze back to the screen, I reached for the last slice of pizza, not noticing that Danny was doing the same. Our hands grazed lightly and I felt a spark of electricity shoot up my arm.

"You have it."

"No, you can have it."

Our hands stayed where they were, lingering over the last slice of pizza. I could feel myself leaning in closer to Danny when someone's phone rang.

"That's yours, Ruby."

Glancing across the room, I saw that he was right. It was probably my mum wanting to know all about the wedding. I abandoned the last slice of pizza and whatever was or wasn't going to happen with Danny and answered my phone. I turned to tell Danny that I was going to take it in the bathroom, to find him half way through eating the last of the pizza. He grinned at me.

"Ya snooze, ya loose!"

I gave him the finger whilst moving into the bathroom to talk to my mum. Honestly, she could have waited like five minutes and not only would I have gotten the last slice but maybe I would have even kissed Danny. Maybe it was a relief that my mum phoned when she did.

I pulled myself back to the conversation with her. We talked about the wedding, the food and the bride's dress. She asked how Danny and his family were.

"Mum, I've got to go. We're watching a film and eating pizza because we had a late-night last night."

No need to mention the copious amounts of drinking.

"The dancing went on until the small hours of the morning with everybody still going strong. At one point, we even did a conga line through the whole hotel."

"OK, honey, enjoy the rest of the weekend. I'll speak to you tomorrow. Tell Danny to drive home safe."

"I will. Love you, Mum."

"Love you too, Ruby."

I hung up the phone and went back into the bedroom. Danny was watching the movie but turned round when I came in.

"I decided to be nice and I have left you half of the last slice."

"And I didn't think you had it in you to be nice."

I got back onto the bed and glancing down noticed the 'half' Danny had left me.

"That isn't half of anything. It's the crust and you know that it's the worst part of the pizza."

"Oh, so you don't want it then?" Danny asked, raising his eyebrow.

"I didn't say that. I'll take any bit of the pizza."

I ate the crust, feeling my hangover ebbing away. No more drinking for a month. Well at least until I went for a night out with Taylor.

"Thank you," Danny said, all his attention focused on me.

"For what?" I said with my mouth still full of pizza.

"For coming with me to the wedding. You made it so much more bearable and I actually had fun. The last family wedding I went to, I had to go stag and the bride's sister kept trying to seduce me."

"I'm glad you asked me. I had fun too."

"Thanks, Ruby, you're a good friend."

I smiled at him, hiding my pain through it. We went back to the movie and whatever moment was going to happen before my mum rang, it was over and firmly in the past. And besides with that last comment, I had just been friend-zoned. He definitely didn't feel the same way about me as I did him.

Chapter 20
15th September

After the wedding, me and Danny resumed our normal routine of working together, trying to avoid the devil in disguise. We hung out after work at his house and mine. He didn't look like he was going to try and kiss me again so I forced it out of my mind.

As September drew closer, I started to prepare for college. I still had one more year left but Danny had already graduated. He was planning on picking up some more shifts at the supermarket and teaching more classes at the pool because he needed the money for university. I couldn't blame him. University was expensive and neither of us wanted to rely on our parents very much. And besides, it gave me another year to spend with him which I couldn't complain about.

Every minute I wasn't spending with Danny, I was hanging out with Taylor. And every time me and Taylor hung out, he pestered me for details about Danny and tried to convince me to stop being a wuss and just ask Danny out. Every time, I laughed and then declined. Declined on both the details and asking out.

At present, Taylor was laying on my bed, flicking through my Instagram and I was trying to complete my English homework for tomorrow. Emphasis on the trying as every five seconds, Taylor would turn the phone around and show me some degrading picture of one of our class mates, usually with a degrading comment from him.

I closed my English book in exasperation and went to lay down on my bed next to Taylor.

"I give up. You are too distracting. I'll just have to do the homework tomorrow morning while you are in your physics class. I've got a free period then anyway."

"Ruby. Weekends were not made for homework and studying. They were made for partying and relaxing. And of course, hanging out with your best friend of all time. And besides, if you hadn't been hanging out with Danny so much, you could have done your homework when I had a shift."

"I wasn't hanging out with Danny. I was working. You know I made sure my shifts were the same as yours so we could hang out more. It just so happens that Danny was on yesterday's shift."

Taylor put the back of his hand to his forehead, feigning hurt and heartbreak.

"I can't believe it has come to this. You're choosing your hoe over your bro."

A fake tear escaped the corner of his eye.

I rolled my eyes.

"With skills like that, it's a wonder why you didn't enrol in the drama program at school."

"But the drama department is just full of geeks and theatre nerds."

"Tay, you're like the biggest theatre nerd I know. I've seen you sing and recite the whole of Annie."

"My dear, Ruby, I'm also an intellectual. Someone who aspires to change the world, not only through toe tapping but through science. Besides, I'm too pretty for theatre."

I shoved his shoulder playfully.

"Whatever helps you sleep at night."

"For your information, I sleep like a baby with a smile on my face."

"For your information, you snore and you only have a smile on your face because you are thinking of ways to torment the people at school."

Taylor laughed darkly.

"Well, the bitches deserve it."

"That they do."

"So, tell me more about the handsome hunk who's taking up all of your free time."

"Well, he is super good looking and we can talk about anything and I really like him but unfortunately he likes laying on my bed, using my phone and eating my snacks."

Taylor paused, a biscuit half way to his mouth.

"I didn't mean me, you silly goose. I was talking about drool worthy Danny."

He put the entire biscuit in his mouth, smirking at me.

"You know how things are going with me and Danny. Nothing has changed. I told you about the nearly almost kiss after the wedding but come to think of it, I may have just imagined it. He didn't mention anything about it when I came off the phone. And he hasn't brought it up since."

He sighed.

"Ruby, we've been over this. You just need to kiss him senseless and show him that you are into him. He would have to be mad or blind not to be into you. Unless of course, he swings for my team in which case I will gladly take him off your hands for you."

"Oh, Tay, you're so kind. Whatever would I do without you?" I muttered sarcastically.

"You would be in dire need of makeover and new clothes and would probably not be as awesome as you are now. What are you doing on Friday? And don't you dare say working because we have a party to go to."

"I guess I'm going to a party then. Whose?"

"Lauren. Well, her boyfriend's party but she's hosting as he doesn't have any brain cells capable of any kind of planning."

"Open house?"

"Yes, but when has that ever stopped us before? The best parties are the ones you aren't invited to."

"True, true."

I nodded, already mentally planning my outfit.

"And you could invite Danny if you wanted to. God knows it would give the bitches at school something to gossip over, you know, him being not a college boy but him being a hot older guy."

"OK, I'll invite him but don't get your hopes up. He may be busy."

Taylor pouted.

"OK fine. Ring me when he says he's coming."

He hauled himself off my bed and out the door.

"I'm going to head home. Mum's cooking lasagne."

"He might not come on Friday!" I yelled after Taylor.

"He will if it means spending more time with you. See you tomorrow."

I sighed. When Taylor was on a mission, nothing would stop him, come hell or high water.

I picked up my phone debating whether to ring or text Danny. It was a Sunday so the pool was closed but he might have picked up another shift at the supermarket. Deciding not to chance it, I pulled up my text messages and found Danny's name. I smiled at our previous messages from a couple of days ago. I had turned up to work and Danny wasn't in our usual meeting place so I had texted him to find out where he was. There was no way he was leaving me to suffer through a shift on my own.

He had responded with a sarcastic 'I'm coming, keep your knickers on straight.'

I loved that Danny could make me laugh with the most unexpected things. And I was so glad that we had gone back into our easy friendship pattern after the wedding, further proof that I had imagined any almost kisses.

I tapped out a message to Danny and re-opened my English book. Now that Taylor had gone home, I could finally concentrate on my homework.

I had written at least half of my essay when my phone buzzed next to me.

What kind of party are we talking about?

I was about to reply when another message came through.

And when?
It's this Friday and it's a keg and pizza kind of thing.

Danny's reply came through after a few minutes. *I would come but I already told my mates that I would go to their beer thing at his uni in Sheffield.*

That's OK. When are you coming back from Sheffield?
Why are you going to miss me?
No of course not. I'm just wondering if I'll be working any shifts on my own at the hell others still stupidly call a supermarket.
I'm coming back on Saturday evening.
I smiled.
I'm not working on Saturday.
I know!

I re-read those two simple words. Did Danny mean that he had deliberately gone to see some of his friends when he knew I wasn't working so that I wouldn't have to work alone? Or was there another reason?

Have fun. Don't do anything I wouldn't do.
Ha! That opens up a lot of possibilities.

I laughed out loud, choosing to ignore Danny's comment.
Turning back to my homework, I let myself get immersed in *Streetcar Named Desire*. Taylor could wait until tomorrow to find out that Danny wasn't coming on Friday.

Chapter 21
3rd November

"If I have to see another advent calendar or another Christmas tree shaped box, I might actually have a mental break down."

"But Christmas is such a magical time. All the lights, the snow and the presents. Not to mention the food."

Danny shook his head at me.

"Ruby, just because there is food, doesn't mean it's a good thing."

"And that's where you are wrong, my friend. Food makes everything better."

We continued putting Christmas chocolates out on the self before, Danny said, "I don't see why shops have to start selling Christmas stuff before Halloween has even passed."

"Chill beans. And besides Christmas is a magical time and we need more time to appreciate it."

He gave me a mocking glance.

"Don't look at me like that."

I turned back to continue stacking the shelves.

"What are you doing for Christmas?"

"My mum always goes all out. She'll start decorating the house from the start of December. She would do it earlier if we let her."

Laughing, I said, "Same. I start decorating as soon as I can. But I think you've guessed that already."

Danny nodded.

Keeping my eyes on the shelf in front of me, I said, "I've already thought of what to get you for Christmas."

"And what is it?"

Hearing the actual curiosity in his voice I felt relieved. That meant he didn't think it was silly to get presents for each other even though we had only known each other for a few months.

"I'm not telling you. It's a surprise."

"Aw come on, don't leave me hanging."

Danny pouted in his incredibly sexy way that nearly made me blurt out all that was on my mind.

"Well, you'll have to wait and see."

"I'll tell you what I'm getting you."

My eyes bounced up to his, delight and intrigue fighting it out in my face. I was nearly tempted but I held my resolve.

"Nope. You'll have to find out at Christmas."

"You're no fun," Danny said, smirking at me.

"I know. But yet you still stick around."

I gave him a teasing poke to the stomach.

Our manager chose that moment to walk round the corner.

"I'm not paying you to stand around and chat. I'm paying you to stock up my shelves."

He glared at us for good measure and turned away, probably to go and smoke outside.

"He really needs to get another job," Danny whispered.

"But if he did then we would have to do actual work," I whispered back.

"What do you mean? I work very hard."

"Um yeah. Sure, you do, Danny. Currently you're still holding the same box of shortbreads you were holding 15 minutes ago."

I folded my arms across my chest, trying to look stern.

"Well at least I'm holding something. You've got nothing in your hands."

"That's because I've just finished stacking the advent calendars."

I gave him a triumphant look, gesturing to the shelves.

Smirking, Danny said, "OK, I believe you."

We continued our shift, chatting away about everything under the sun. I couldn't wait to go Christmas shopping and get Danny's gift. He was going to love it. I had found a vintage record of his favourite album in an old record store that wasn't too far away. Me and Taylor were heading into town in a couple of weeks to get presents for everyone.

My whole thought process put a happy shimmer on the rest of my shift. I loved Christmas so much and nothing could stop that feeling.

Chapter 22
13th December

This is a marvellous day. We had finally come to the end of the term. Thankfully my teachers hadn't given me much Christmas work to do so that meant I could relax with Taylor and Danny and pick up some more shifts. I mean, who doesn't love money to spend on clothes, books and shoes?

As it was the last day of school, one of the bimbos was throwing the obligatory end of term party which me and Taylor were obviously going to. A party was a party, no matter if the host was a bitch.

"I'm wearing my leopard print jeans with that black top you made me buy last weekend."

"Tay, I didn't make you buy anything. You said it was your Christmas present to yourself."

"I'm allowed to treat myself every now and again."

"Yeah, but not every weekend," I muttered under my breath.

"Do you want me to drive your stupid ass into town tomorrow or are you going to keep making sarcastic comments?"

"You're not driving. Your mum is."

I pointed out. Taylor had passed his driving test months ago but couldn't afford a car yet so we still had to rely on the bus and our parents.

"Just because I'm not part of the elite few who get a car just for turning 17."

He huffed, drawing his coat further around himself as we waited for the bus. He glared at a pink car zooming past.

"Well, I like our bonding time on the bus. And we get to terrorise the younger students."

"And you know how much I like terrorising idiots."

Taylor grinned.

"Back to the party, what are you wearing?"

"That red dress we found a couple of weeks ago. With a Santa hat."

"And those tall 'take me to bed' boots," added Taylor.

"I'm not planning on taking anyone to bed at this party, you know."

"Yes, but they make you look absolutely stunning. And sexy."

Taylor winked at me.

"Honey, if I was a straight man, I would do you in those boots in a heartbeat."

I threw my arm around Taylor's shoulder.

"You fill me with such confidence."

He grinned at me.

"OK fine, I'll wear the boots."

"Good. We need to make a lasting impression on these bitches. Wouldn't want to leave them thinking that we are complete morons."

"Hell yeah! And then what time are we leaving tomorrow?"

"Definitely not any earlier than 11 a.m. I'm planning on getting trashed tonight."

I nodded. Our bus came round the corner and we got on, claiming our seats. We were heading back to mine for a bit. My mum was cooking pizza and I needed to get ready for the party and then we were going to head over to Taylor's house. My mum knew we were going to a house party tonight and was more than happy for me to stay at Taylor's. She preferred it, if I'm honest, because then she didn't have to worry about me waking up my sisters.

The bus stopped by my house and we got off. I opened my front door and both me and Taylor walked in. Taylor went straight to the kitchen, finding the snacks and my mum.

"Hey, mum!" I yelled out from the hall. "When are the pizzas going to be ready?"

"They will be ready at 6!" Mum yelled back.

Taylor followed me up to my room with a plate of fresh brownies my mum had just made.

"How did you get those? Mum would have never given them to me."

"Well honey, your mum actually likes me. I mean, who wouldn't? I am fabulous."

With that he flicked his head back as if he sported waist length hair and was flicking that back.

"I'm glad you grabbed them. I'm starving."

"Who said any of these are for you?"

"Tay, it's my house. Therefore, I get the snacks."

Scoffing the still warm brownies, I threw some clothes and essentials into a bag while Taylor laid out my red dress.

"I'm going to have to change at yours. Mum knows we're going out but she doesn't know about the dress and if she saw me in it, she would never let me leave."

"Ha true. But you look super-hot in it so you have to wear it."

I packed the dress as well as the boots, leaving my converse shoes out to keep my mother's suspicions away. We flopped on to my bed and put a film on to pass the time until the pizzas were ready.

****

Waking up after a night of heavy drinking was never pretty. My eyes reluctantly opened to the sun shining through Taylor's curtains. I heard Tay groaning next to me, grumbling about something incoherent.

"Come on, wake up. We have to get into town."

I slapped his arm with each word.

"Let me sleep. Just five more minutes."

"I want to sleep my hangover off as well but we need to get into town. We have Christmas presents to buy."

He groaned again but started pushing himself up ready to slither out of bed.

"We are so stopping at Costa first. I need coffee if you expect my normal perky self."

An hour later, we were standing in line at Costa, waiting for our extra-large coffees to be made and Taylor was cramming a cinnamon bun into his mouth.

"I don't see how you can even think about eating, especially after last night."

I pulled a face at the sweet icing and pungent cinnamon.

"Darling, it's simple really. You open your mouth, put the food inside and chew."

Taylor demonstrated this by shoving another large bite into his mouth.

"You're gross!"

"I know but you love me anyway," he said, grinning at me.

"You've got me there."

I grabbed our coffees and we made our way out of the store.

"Where first?"

"I need to get the 'rentals' something so like somewhere posh. But cheap. I'm not made of money."

"I think what you mean, Tay, is that you want more money to spend on your best friend in the whole world's Christmas present."

"That's where you are definitely mistaken. I want more money to spend on my awesome self."

He winked at me before linking his arm through mine.

"Come, wench, the shops await."

We went into half a dozen or so shops and brought presents for our parents and my sisters. I found a new eye shadow palette for Ciara and some boots for Ella. Taylor and I were seeing *Wicked* the musical in London in the new year which was our Christmas present to each other. It had been our tradition, dinner and a show, for as long as we had known each other. Obviously, we started going with our parents but for the last few years, we had been going just the two of us.

"So, what are you getting for Danny? Are you finally going to ask him out so your gift can, be you?"

He placed an overly large bow on my head and wiggled his eyebrows in a comic fashion.

"Do I need to get you something else for Christmas like condoms and lacy underwear?"

"Taylor, if you so much as let your filthy brain go down that road again, I will hurt you so much."

"Yeah, I'd like to see your short-ass take on all of this."

He gestured to his impressive height and, I'll admit it, amazing abs.

"So, if sex is off the table, what are you getting Danny?"

"I found a record of his favourite album. And the cover art looks amazing."

Taylor gave me a quizzical look.

"Honey, I think you should stick with jumping his bones. Who even owns a record player anymore?"

"Well, Danny doesn't."

Before Taylor could interject with another sarcastic comment I added, "He just collects them and frames them. But he only collects the ones with really good or rare cover art. Which is why this one is perfect."

"I'm still thinking the lacy underwear will definitely be better. And think of it as a present for him not for you."

Instead of justifying that comment with a response, I simply gave him my 'fuck off' look.

"OK fine. Get the record. But trust me, if he had the choice, he would definitely choose my idea."

"I'm going with the record and besides there is no way of finding out which option he would prefer. I can't really go up to him and say 'hey do you want a record or my body for Christmas?'"

"Honey, there ain't anything stopping you doing exactly that."

I just sighed. It was too complicated to get into now.

We continued our shopping, buying ourselves a few Christmas presents on the side and left to go get some food.

Chapter 23
Later That Day

After Taylor's mum had dropped me off at my house, I made some little gingerbread men and while they cooked, I quickly wrapped all my presents. This way, I could leave them all under the tree and wouldn't have to worry about storing them in my small room or anyone peeking in the carrier bags.

Once the cookies had cooled, I iced them, giving them each a slightly different look and personality. Taylor always teased me about doing this but I couldn't care less. Each cookie was like a different person in my eyes. And Taylor still managed to scoff plenty down his throat. These gingerbread men however, were for Danny and his family as I was heading over to his house in about an hour.

Since I didn't know Danny's family all too well, I had decided to play it safe and stick with cookies and not get them something which they wouldn't like. And not to brag, but my gingerbread could make grown men weep with happiness.

I placed them in a box I had found in town. It had a cute snowman design, with little snow-dogs running around and a wrapped ribbon round it, making a bow on top.

I grabbed my boots and coat, dashing into the bathroom to double check my hair and outfit. I had one of my many

Christmas jumpers on and candy cane earrings swinging from my ears. I even had my lucky Christmas underwear on, not that anyone was going to see that.

"Bye, Ella, bye, Ciara, I'm heading out."

I listened to the pin-drop silence but as usual, there was no response even though I knew that both my sisters were in the house.

"There's a gingerbread man on the counter for each of you."

Still no response but mum was coming back from her shift at the hospital soon anyway.

I carefully placed Danny's present in my handbag, grabbed the box of cookies and locked the door behind me. Danny only lived a few streets away so I could walk it in five minutes.

When I got to Danny's house, I rang the doorbell. If I was going to Taylor's house, I would just waltz in and plonk myself down on the sofa. Since I had only been friends with Danny for a few months, I decided against just walking in so I stood in the freezing cold, waiting for someone to open the door.

Rosetta answered.

"Hi, honey. Merry Christmas."

"Merry Christmas."

I stepped in and she shut the door behind me.

"These are for you and the family. I'd open it now because it's homemade and I don't want them to go off."

"Oh, you shouldn't have."

Danny's mum took the box and lifted the lid. The smell of ginger immediately filled the entrance hall.

"These smell gorgeous. And you say they are homemade?"

"Yeah, made them fresh this afternoon."

"I might have to keep these a secret from the others and eat them all myself."

She took them through to the kitchen, already munching one.

"Danny's in his room. Here take some cookies up to him before I eat them all."

She thrust a plate at me, holding the legs of one gingerbread man in her other hand.

"These are delicious, dear."

"Thanks. I'll see you in a bit."

I took my boots and coat off and walked up the stairs. I had been here quite a few times since becoming friends with Danny, so I was familiar with the layout of his house and knew where his room was, a fact that Taylor said I should use to sneak into his house to jump his bones.

Coming to Danny's door, I knocked and pushed the door open. Danny was lying in bed, watching an action movie. He looked my way at the sound of the door opening and smiled.

"Merry Christmas," he said, moving over on his bed so I could lay down next to him.

"Merry Christmas."

I put the plate down on his bed.

"I made these for your family and your mum said to take some up for you before she ate the whole lot."

"I thought I could smell something good."

He picked one up and put the whole thing in his mouth at once.

"Holy mother, these are amazing."

He was already picking up another one, his mouth barely empty from the last one.

"Pace yourself, there's a whole box downstairs."

I smiled to myself. It was always a compliment when someone enjoyed my cooking.

"Nah, my parents have probably demolished half the box by now. Do you want to continue this movie or watch a Christmas film?"

"Obviously a Christmas film. It is December after all."

Before Danny could say another word, I pulled out 3 disks from my bag, all Christmas themed films.

"Oh wow, you've come prepared."

"Only because I knew you didn't have any Christmas films and I didn't want to take a chance with whatever is on the TV."

Danny chose a film and put it into the DVD player.

"Don't put your film in my Christmas case. You know I hate that."

He put the action film in the correct case. I didn't see the title, something to do with cars and he put the Christmas film in.

"I love *The Santa Clause*," I told him as he sat back on the bed. "And you're in luck because this is a three-part film series."

"And let me guess, you have all three."

"Of course, I do. I brought them together a couple of years ago. It would be silly to buy one and not the others."

"Yeah, so silly."

Danny rolled his eyes at me.

"When you thrust the Christmas trash upon me, I may have noticed a present in your bag."

"It's a shame, because it's not for you." I teased, taking a gingerbread man. "It's for my other friend who keeps me sane at work."

He put his hand to his heart.

"I didn't realise you had other friends."

I punched his arm.

"I have other friends."

"Sure."

"Fine, I'll just take these cookies to my other friends then." I started getting of the bed, meaning to take the plate away before Danny grabbed my wrist and pulled me back.

"Don't you dare take these delicious cookies away from me."

I settled back down on to the bed and smiled at him.

"I wouldn't dare. The present is for you though."

"That's good. Do you want yours then?"

"Yes of course I do."

I felt my grin splitting my face but I couldn't help it, I loved getting and receiving presents.

"Can we open them now? I want to see your reaction to your present."

"Sure."

He leaned down and pulled a package out from under his bed.

"I'll be honest, Stella wrapped it. I can't wrap presents to save my life."

"I know, my birthday present looked like it had been wrapped by a child."

Laughing, I pulled out Danny's present from my bag.

"I'll be honest, I wrapped this myself, because I am an adult."

"Ha-ha," he said. "Here you go."

We traded presents and I looked expectantly at Danny.

"Aren't you going to open it?" he asked.

"No, I'm going to watch you open yours first. I told you I want to see your face."

"OK. Suit yourself."

He pulled off the paper and flipped the record over.

"Oh, Ruby. It's amazing. I love it."

His face had lit up as his eyes roamed over all aspects of the cover and the song list on the back.

"I'm glad you like it. You can add it to your collection."

"I think I might have to just stare at it for a bit first."

He turned to me.

"Open yours now."

I slipped my finger under the Sellotape and pulled the paper away from the present. I gasped. In my hands, I held the first edition copies of the *Narnia* book set.

"Danny, how did you find this? I searched everywhere for copies."

"I have my secrets."

I glared at him.

"OK fine, last month when we were visiting my aunt, there was a second-hand book shop that specialised in older books. So, I went in trying to find something for you and saw this."

I threw my arms around his shoulders, keeping hold of the books in one hand.

"Thank you so much, Danny."

He returned the hug, his arms slipping around my waist as though they belong there. We stayed hugging for a little longer and I felt my defences start to slip.

"Let's watch the movie," I said, jumping out of Danny's arms.

"Um yeah, lets."

We turned our attention to the screen, losing ourselves in the film.

If I had stayed in Danny's arms for much longer, I would have surely kissed him. And we would need a Christmas miracle to make our friendship go beyond that.

Chapter 24
14th February

I hated Valentine's Day with a passion. OK, I didn't hate it, I just didn't like the fact that I never managed to hold down a boyfriend long enough to get to Valentine's Day. Taylor always surprised me with some nice chocolates and a cute present but it wasn't the same.

Although, Taylor was the only consistent guy in my life at the moment.

"I know that you are working tonight but it would be so romantic for you to express your feelings for Danny. Just imagine it, standing in the canned goods aisle, professing your love for one another."

Taylor's voice came floating through my daydream, causing me to look up with a start.

"The only acceptable answer for that gushy look on your face, is that you were thinking about a certain hunk at the supermarket."

I quickly rearranged my face.

"I wasn't looking gushy."

"Babe, you so were. It's like a beacon for the lonely."

I pushed him and returned to my English essay. Teachers really shouldn't give homework due for Valentine's Day. It was just cruel.

My phone buzzed and I pulled it out, thinking it might be Danny. To my disappointment, it was Craig. I put my phone down without even unlocking it, let alone replying.

"Who was that?"

"Just Craig."

I showed Taylor the text and he scowled in response.

"I can't believe you slept with someone called Craig. I thought you had better taste than that."

"Well, I was drunk, what can I say? And it was a one-time thing."

"It had better be. You can do so much better, girlfriend."

"I know. And between you and me," I leaned towards Taylor so I couldn't be overheard, "His junk is very small."

Taylor threw his head back and laughed, making some other students turn around and stare at us in disgust for breaking the sacred silence of the library.

Recovering his posture, Taylor said, "You know, I bet Danny's…"

I slapped my hand over his mouth before he could finish that sentence. I knew exactly where his filthy mind had taken him and I needed no more encouraging to think about Danny's package.

"Shh, Tay, we are in a library."

He gave me a pointed look and raised his eyebrows.

"Now if I remove my hand, promise you won't bring up Danny again. Or any part of him."

Taylor nodded and I moved my hand away before he felt inclined to lick it like we used to do as kids.

"I still can't believe you slept with Craig."

Taylor shook his head as though trying to rid himself of the image.

"Honestly, I wasn't going to sleep with him but then things just happened. If it makes you feel any better, I didn't stay at his house afterwards. He fell asleep very quickly and I went back home."

"Good. Because that's an essential rule for one-night stands."

"True that."

I deleted the text and we went back to moaning about school, work and the annoying bitches at our school.

Chapter 25
3rd March

Last week had come as a blessing. It was half term week which meant a week off school. Me and Taylor had gone to the essential last day of term party at some slut's house and had gotten drunk off our asses. I had picked up more shifts over the week because who wants to start revising for exams which were coming up in June?

When school had started back up, I had gone back to my normal working schedule and started opening relevant textbooks to fool my mum into thinking I was revising.

However, today was a Friday, which meant me and Danny were working from 4 until closing time at 10:30. This was always a good shift because Danny walked me home afterwards.

Today's shift had started as every other shift had started. I had pulled on my horrible uniform top with black jeans and trudged to the supermarket. Me and Danny a few months ago had given up on the shop regulated trousers as they were disgusting and had started wearing jeans. So far, the manager either didn't care or didn't notice.

I had become quite good at pushing my feelings for Danny down so they didn't affect our friendship. Me and Danny being in a relationship just wasn't on the cards, no matter how much I dreamt of it.

However, things changed today. We were pretending to stack the shelves, and I mean very loosely pretending. I was sitting on the floor, just holding some random bread. Our eyes met when he turned to face me and something sparked between us. I felt like I was drowning in his clear blue eyes and that I could stare at them all day.

And then he asked me out. And he was nervous, as though he had been building up to asking me for some time.

After replying yes, I turned back to my shelf, a wide grin resting on my face. I couldn't wait for tomorrow. I would have to ring Taylor tonight and tell him and I could already imagine the squealing.

Sighing, I went back to my work.

At the end of our shift, Danny walked me home as usual. It was a little awkward between us so we mainly just stayed quiet. When we reached my house, Danny caught my hand and leaned in, giving me a quick and slightly sloppy kiss.

"See you tomorrow."

He hurried off, waving behind him.

I watched him go and then let myself into the house, locking it behind me. My phone was already pressed against my ear, ready to give Taylor the details.

"You do know that I have only just gotten out of the shower, Ruby. Honestly, it's like you have secret cameras in my house."

"Oh damn. You've found them. Now I'll have to move them."

I moved upstairs as I spoke, taking of my clothes and shoes as I went.

I pulled on my PJs and flopped down onto my bed.

"Is there any particular reason you have interrupted my night time beauty routine?"

"If you're going to be grumpy about it, I won't tell you that Danny kissed me today."

As predicted, Taylor squealed loud enough to have all the neighbourhood dogs barking.

"FINALLY. Tell me everything. When? Where? How was it?"

I told Taylor what happened, leaving no details out.

"And then he walked me home as usual and kissed me on the doorstep."

"Yes, girl, finally! What are you going to wear? You don't want to look like you are trying too hard but then you can't wear something you have already worn in front of him. We should really go shopping…" Taylor kept talking and I laid on my bed with a big goofy grin on my face.

"I need something sexy and cute. Something that says 'date'."

"You should definitely wear your black jeans, the ones that make your butt look amazing. And that halter neck top we found on sale last week. It's been really warm for this time of year so you should make the most of it."

"Tay, I love you. What would I do without you?"

"And don't take a jumper, let him give you his if you do get cold."

"Thanks, Tay."

"Ring me tomorrow with all the details."

I hung up and proceeded to grin up at the ceiling for a good hour before drifting off to sleep.

Chapter 26
4th March

I was awoken by my sister Ella screaming up the stairs that she was going out to her friend's house. As I knew Ciara was already up and revising, I let her reply. I was about to pull the covers over my head and go back to sleep when the events of last evening came crashing back to me. I was going on a date. With Danny. I pinched myself to make sure I wasn't dreaming and upon feeling the slight sting, I hopped out of bed and got in the shower.

I took my time, making sure my makeup was perfect but not to heavy and that my hair fell nice and straight down my back. I decided to leave it loose, making it look more natural even though I had just spent half an hour straightening it. Danny didn't need to see my thick curls that were impossible to manage.

I put on my Taylor approved outfit and was just slipping on my ballet flats when the doorbell rang. I heard Ciara get up to answer it and I headed downstairs.

"Hey, you look amazing."

Danny smiled at me, fidgeting slightly on the doorstep.

"These are for you."

He held out some flowers.

"Thanks. I'll just put them in some water."

Taking them from him, I headed into the kitchen.

"I'm going over to my friend's house to study. I won't be back until tomorrow morning. Mum knows," Ciara said to me, not looking up from her text book.

"OK. And Ella's staying over at her friend's house, right?"

Ciara looked up at me briefly and nodded.

"I'm going out with Danny. Make sure you lock the door behind you."

I headed back to the door, grabbing my bag on the way.

"Let's go."

We walked to his car and drove off to the river. We chatted a bit but there was tension and sexual chemistry mounting as we spoke.

Reaching the carpark by the river, we got out and headed off towards the less populated walk. Dog walkers came here all the time but they always went towards the right so we took the left-hand path.

We walked along the path, chatting about college, work and our families. Stopping at a bridge, I leant over the railing, feeling Danny stand next to me as our arms brushed. I felt a spark of electricity shoot between us, making me sure that this date wouldn't be a disaster.

"It's beautiful here, isn't it?"

"Yes beautiful."

I turned to look at Danny but finding his gaze already on me. I blushed slightly and pushed off the bridge.

Before I could start walking, Danny said, "I like your hair like that."

"Um thanks. I'll let you in on a secret. It's not natural. My natural hair is super curly."

He caught a stand between his fingers and started curling it round his forefinger.

"So, if I kept doing this would it make your hair go curly?"

I unconsciously stepped forward towards him.

"Maybe. But I spent ages on it this morning so you had better stop."

"I'll stop if you kiss me."

I looked up to his eyes, seeing the dare twinkling there. I leant up and placed my lips lightly on his, giving him the quickest peck.

But before I could pull away, Danny had one hand on my hip and the other cradling my head, pulling me closer and moulding our lips together. I lifted my arms and slid them around his neck, holding him firmly in place. Our mouths explored each other's and I felt my knees go weak and butterflies erupt in my stomach.

Danny pulled back and rested his forehead against mine, both of us breathing heavily and our breath mingling in the small space between our lips.

"I've been wanting to do that for some time," he whispered.

I responded by pulling his head back down and kissing him again, letting the kiss speak of my feelings.

Separating at last, Danny said, "We should continue along the river bank."

"I've got a better idea," I said, linking our hands together and pulling him back to the car.

We arrived back at mine and I unlocked the door.

"Are you sure there is no one home?"

I turned around and kissed him.

"Just us."

He kissed me back, kicking the door closed behind him. We stayed in the hall, our mouths exploring. Danny's mouth left a trail of kisses down my neck and across my collar. I felt his mouth go lower and lower. I fisted my hands through his hair and pulled his mouth back up to mine.

Pulling apart, I took his hand and led him up the stairs to my bedroom. I shut the door behind us, kissing him again before the door had finished shutting. I started undoing his shirt buttons, his hands pulling out my belt. I stopped kissing Danny to quickly pull my shirt over my head and he responded in kind by finishing with the buttons and discarding his shirt. I wiggled out of my jeans while he toed of his shoes and socks.

Having thrown my jeans on the floor, I backed towards the bed, holding Danny's gaze. He quickly followed, ripping his jeans of as he came toward me. Danny kissed me again and I put my hands round his neck, pulling him down on top of me. Our underwear came off and I felt Danny's gaze travel up and down my body, his fingers stroking a path that seared itself onto my skin.

"Danny." I begged. "I need you now."

He slid a condom on and with a grunt, pushed into me. I wrapped my legs around his waist as he set a hard, fast rhythm, stroking in and out of me.

"Danny!" I screamed. "I'm close."

Danny kissed me again, pushing into me again and again.

I felt my orgasm building up and bit down on Danny's shoulder just as I felt my release. Danny followed, collapsing down on top of me. He pulled out and wrapped the condom and threw it in the bin.

He turned to me.

"Well, that wasn't how I saw today playing out."

"I don't care. I'm glad it happened."

While speaking, I started trailing my fingers up and down Danny's chest. I let my eyes roam over his chest and abs, going lower and lower with my fingers following my eyes.

My fingers encircled his dick. Taylor was right, Danny's package was definitely bigger that Craig's. Way bigger. My fingers squeezed lightly and I felt Danny harden. I pushed him over onto his back and straddled my leg over his lap. He caught my lips in a fiery embrace as I leaned down over him.

I reached for a condom from my night stand and slid it over Danny. I ran my hands over his chest and lifting my hips slightly, I dropped back down, sliding myself onto his thick shaft.

I arched my back, relishing in the feel of him inside of me. With one hand, Danny held my hip as I bucked on top of him. With the other hand, he let it travel over my stomach and up to my boobs, where he tweaked first one nipple and then the other. He sat up, pulling me closer and took one breast into his mouth, his tongue doing wicked things to me.

Feeling myself nearing my release, I pulled Danny's mouth back up to mine and melded our lips together, each of us taking in the other's scream.

Chapter 27
Later on That Day

Me and Danny dressed ourselves and then Danny quickly left, saying he had to go to work. I saw him out, he gave me a quick peck on the lips and got into his car without a backwards glance.

I closed the door behind him and sat against it. Pulling out my phone, I called Taylor.

"Come over right now. It's an emergency."

10 minutes later Taylor walked into my house with cookie dough ice cream and a hug. He went and got two spoons and we sat and ate ice cream out of the tub.

"If that bastard hurt you in anyway, I'm going to kill him."

"He didn't. He picked me up and we went down the quieter path along the river. We had such a lovely walk and we flirted a bit. And then he kissed me. Like I think my heart stopped for a second there."

I looked down and started fiddling with my shirt.

"And then we came back here and slept together."

Taylor dropped his spoon.

"You slept together!"

"Twice."

I grinned at him.

"It was wonderful but then he left really quickly afterwards saying he had to get to work."

Taylor put his arms around me.

I hugged Taylor back.

"It's OK. We had amazing sex and now we will probably go back to being friends. It's better to just put this whole episode behind me."

"You never know, he might come to his senses and come back."

"I don't think so, Tay."

"Well at least you've had some good sex to clean out your system."

I laughed. Taylor always knew just what to say to me. We finished the ice cream and put on *Bridget Jones's Diary* and I let any thoughts of Danny vanish from my mind.

****

The following morning, I woke up to my sister Ella shaking my shoulder.

"Wake up, there's someone at the door for you."

"If its Taylor, tell him to go away and come back later."

I rolled over, pulling the duvet over my head.

"It's not Taylor, it's that guy you work with."

I sat up.

"What?"

"The guy you work with is standing at our front door and he's asking for you."

I shot out of bed and ran down the stairs. Danny was leaning against the door frame, scrolling through his phone with one hand and the other hand causally sticking out of his pocket.

He glanced up at me when he heard my footsteps.

"Hi."

"What are you doing here?"

Danny's eyes raked my body and glancing down I realised I was still in my PJs. Well, if you can call shorts and a tank top PJ.

Danny brought his eyes back up to my face and said, "Yesterday, we ended things badly. What I wanted to ask you was would you be my girlfriend?"

I stared back dumbfounded.

"But you left so suddenly after... after... you know."

"After we had sex, you mean."

His eyes twinkled.

I couldn't get my jaw to work. I just stood there staring at Danny who stepped closer to me.

"You still haven't answered my question."

He put his hands on my waist and started kissing my jaw, light, barely there kisses.

"Will you be my girlfriend?"

He punctuated each word with a feather-light kiss, each time getting closer to my lips.

I brought my hands up to his shoulders.

"Yes."

Danny pulled back slightly.

"Really?"

"Yes, now kiss me."

Danny obliged and our lips met, sparks flying. His hands around my waist, pulled me in closer and my hands gripped his shoulders as though my life depended on it.

We pulled apart and before Danny could kiss me again, I said, "But you left yesterday so quickly. I thought I had done something wrong or that you just wanted sex."

He cupped his hands round my face, forcing me to look into his eyes.

"I really had to work. I didn't realise the time. And all the time I was teaching kids to swim, I just wanted to drive over here, apologise and take you back to bed."

I kissed him again.

"I would invite you back to my bed but both my sisters and my mum are home."

I kissed him again.

"So, girlfriend, shall we go to the movies tomorrow?"

"Yes, boyfriend, we should."

He grinned and kissed me again. He left and I closed the door and I floated back upstairs on cloud 9.

Chapter 28
20th April

Things between me and Danny were good. In fact, they were better than good. We still worked together but now we stole quick but passionate kisses here and there. Every time we hung out together, it was amazing. And the sex. Well, let's just say, Danny knows how to keep a girl satisfied.

As it was the week after the Easter holidays, I was trying to keep up with college work and revision.

Currently, I was sitting in the library, trying to work but Taylor kept talking my ear off. I couldn't blame him; he was planning our birthday party. We always did something together as his birthday was two days after mine. We've done the whole range from a bouncy castle in the back garden to a holiday in France. This year, as we were turning 18, Taylor was planning a huge party. His parents were going to be out of town that weekend so it was the perfect opportunity to throw a party.

"I mean I would love to have a pamper evening, getting our nails done while watching *Princess Diaries* but society dictates that we throw a massive rager and invite all the bitches we know."

"Well, we can have a pamper evening the day before so we are ready to kick ass at our party."

Taylor nodded.

"I definitely need that. What with the stress of exams getting to me. Are you inviting Danny?"

"I wasn't going to. We are doing something the day before my birthday. I don't know what though. Danny said it's a surprise."

"Well, you should invite him to our party."

Taylor started tapping on his phone.

"Fine, I'll ask him."

"Good. Now I need your playlist and what you are planning on wearing so we can coordinate. It would be a disaster if we clashed with each other and the décor."

I simply nodded. When Taylor was in party mode, he was unreachable. He had always planned all of our birthdays and they were always amazing. Sometimes he didn't need me to do more than nod a few times at the right moments.

Picking up my phone, I opened my messages between me and Danny and tapped out a message to him.

So, for my birthday…

Danny replied before I could type another message.

I'm not telling you where I'm taking you xx
I was not going to ask, again xx
Sure, you weren't xx
Me and Taylor are throwing a party for our joint birthdays. Do you want to come?
Sure xx

It's the weekend after my birthday xx
I'll meet you at your house xx

"What's got that goofy expression on your face for?"

Taylor looked up from his phone to see me grinning like the Cheshire cat.

"Danny's coming to the party. He's going to meet me at mine and we'll walk across together. I'll come over to yours to help set up and then head back to mine to meet Danny."

"OK cool. What are you going to wear?"

"Tay, I don't know. It's like three weeks away."

Taylor sighed.

"Ruby, have I taught you nothing? You should always plan an outfit for a big event at least a month in advance."

I racked my brains, trying to think of what clothes I owned.

Seeing my hesitation, Taylor said, "We'll have to go shopping. I can see by the look on your face that you have nothing to wear. And besides, you can't wear something from your tragic wardrobe."

"Fine. We can go afterschool sometime."

I went back to my revision while Taylor looked through my Spotify playlist. I don't know why he even bothered since our playlists were virtually the same. But every so often, he would come across a song and add it to his list.

Chapter 29
21st May

A couple of hours ago, me and Taylor had stood on his doorstep and waved his parents off. They were going on a romantic break for the weekend so the house was ours. We headed back inside, stared decorating and made the house party ready.

Just before 8, I was dressed and just putting a finishing touch to my makeup.

"I'm heading back to mine to meet Danny. I'll see you in a bit."

I walked the couple of streets back to mine to see Danny lounging against the wall. My phone buzzed in my back pocket with a text from Danny to say he was outside my house.

"Hey handsome."

I encircled his waist and pecked his lips.

"Hey beautiful."

He leant in to kiss me again but I put a hand against his chest.

"Makeup."

He pouted.

"But I want to kiss my gorgeous girlfriend senseless."

"Later, I promise."

Taking his hand, I said, "Shall we go? It's only round the corner."

We walked off, hand in hand towards Taylor's house. There were people already pouring out of the front door, cups in hand and music pumping loud enough to wake the dead.

"Come on let's go."

As I pulled Danny through the door, I greeted a few people. They were already too drunk to care or notice anything beyond their cups. That was one of the few benefits to parties like this, everyone got wasted pretty quickly and didn't remember that they hated me and Taylor.

"Shall we get a drink?" I asked Danny.

He just nodded in response and we found our way to the kitchen.

In the kitchen we bumped into some girl from my English class.

"Let's do shots!"

She pushed a glass into my hand and one into Danny's. We clinked glasses and downed them in one.

"Come on, let's go dance," I said to Danny.

I pushed my way through people until we reached the living room. Taylor had hooked up his impressive speaker system and music was blaring out. People were grinding and dancing on our makeshift dance floor.

I looped my arms round Danny's neck and he pulled me closer. We danced, kissed and drank. I kept catching glimpses of Taylor but he was always gone before I could grab hold of him.

On a drink break in the kitchen, Danny turned to me.

"This is an impressive house."

"I know. I've spent many happy hours here in my childhood."

I took his hand.

"Come, I'll give you the tour. Tay won't mind."

Thankfully, before the party, we had blocked the stairs off. Everything that a party needed was downstairs and this way, we wouldn't have people rummaging through Taylor's room and his parent's room.

Once me and Danny reached the end of the hall, I opened the door to the attic stairs.

"Up here is mine and Taylor's 'secret' cave where we spent most of our time as children."

We climbed the stairs and Danny took in the room that me and Taylor had worked so hard to make perfect.

"Would it be wrong if I kissed you here?"

His arms snaked around my waist, pulling me back against his chest.

"I can't think why you shouldn't."

He spun me around in his arms and planted his lips on mine. I moved my own in sync with his and felt his growing erection poke at my stomach. My hands found their way to his shirt buttons and started pulling them apart.

He broke the kiss.

"We can't have sex in your friend's house. Let alone in your childhood den."

"Would it help if I said we also spent most of our teen years up here as well."

My hands kept undoing buttons as I spoke. I pushed the shirt off his chest and kissed him again.

"Make love to me, Danny."

He needed no further encouragement, joining our lips together. His hands found the hem of my dress and pushed it up, his hands cupping my butt briefly before continuing their journey.

He drew my dress over my head and lifted me off my feet. I wrapped my legs round his waist, leaving no space between us. He dropped his head to my boobs, taking one nipple in his mouth while his hand tweaked the other.

I threw my head back as Danny's mouth pressed hot kisses to my chest and up my throat. My hands went to his jeans and started fiddling with the belt. Finally, his belt came loose and with it the jeans. He wiggled his trousers down his legs as he settled me against the old sofa. He shed his boxers and I rid myself of my knickers. Danny came towards me but stopped when he was an arm's length away from me.

"What?" I said, my eyes searching his.

"You're so beautiful, Ruby. I love you."

"I love you too."

I kissed him, bringing him to lay fully on top of me. He kissed me back, saying 'I love you' without words. He pulled back slightly, our lips still joined and he slid into me. I gasped, loving the feel of his familiar hardness inside me.

Danny started moving, pushing in and out of me, my hips meeting his every thrust, keeping up with his rhythm.

"Danny." I panted.

I wrapped my legs round his waist, anchoring him to me as I felt him tremble inside of me, knowing he was close as well.

"Ruby."

He sighed my name and I felt his release milliseconds before my own. Danny collapsed on top of me and we lay there trying to catch our breath.

He gently pulled out of me and rolled us over so we were laying side by side, wrapped in each other's arms. I could still hear the faint pulsing of the music downstairs but right now I didn't care about that. I only cared about the wonderful man whose arms were wrapped round mine.

We laid like that for hours, or what felt like hours, just talking about anything and everything.

"I love you so much," I whispered to Danny.

"I love you too."

He tightened his grip on me, empathising his words.

We finally got up off the sofa and got dressed. My hair was completely irreparable and one of Danny's shirt buttons had come clean off but apart from that, nothing looked out of the ordinary. I cleaned up the room, straightening sofa cushions and righting the blanket. Me and Danny went back down to the party and danced the rest of the night away.

Chapter 30
22nd May

The morning after dawned bright and annoying. Taylor had forgotten to close the living room curtains so the sun light was streaming in, making my head pound. Honestly, I hadn't even drunk that much.

I lifted my head, finding Taylor asleep on the other end of the sofa. I kicked his leg, trying to wake him. He just grunted in return. I hauled myself off the sofa and went in search of a glass of water and some paracetamol. Having found some, I took a glass back to Taylor who was sitting up and looking around the living room.

He took the glass and pills from me and drank the whole thing down in one.

"Wow I needed that."

He looked at me.

"Honey, you really need a shower. You look gross."

I knew from experience that my face now resembled a clown's mask but shrugged it off. It was only Taylor here after all.

"Have you seen yourself in a mirror recently? You don't look too hot yourself."

He scowled at me.

"Well, you go and shower. I'm going to lay here for a bit more."

After both of us showering and changing into something comfier, we started clearing the used cups and empty bottles from the house.

"Hey, where did you disappear of to last night? One minute you were grinding away on your beefcake and then you had both disappeared."

Taylor raised his eyebrow at me.

"I hope you weren't getting naked in my house."

"Noooo! Of course, we weren't."

I laughed nervously. I went back to picking up empty beer bottles from the floor, trying to avoid Taylor's gaze.

"You did. I know that look."

Taylor narrowed his eyes at me.

"You'd better not have done it in my bed."

"Ha don't worry. We definitely stayed clear of your bedroom."

Seeing his face and where his questioning was going, I added, "and not your parents' room either."

"Well regardless of where you did it, honey you're glowing."

"I know, it's so cliché but ever since my birthday, when we said we loved each other, me and Danny have just been so much more in sync with each other."

"Take that love sick look off your face and start cleaning. Some of us are still single you know." He pouted.

I threw a plastic cup at him which he ducked just in time for.

"I can't believe we are finally 18!" I grinned at Taylor. "We can drink, vote and get married."

Taylor simply gestured to the room, littered with cups, bottles and rubbish.

"I think we already have one of those covered sweet cheeks."

"Yes, and we've got that one down to a fine art by now."

We high-fived each other, grinning like idiots.

"As we are both boycotting prom, as it's expensive and filled with annoying bitches, we should do something special."

"I totally agree. The day of our last exam is next week and the weather's been getting nicer and nicer."

Taylor grinned.

"I know, let's go to the outdoor pool, spend the day. Just the two of us and then we can gate crash a party in the evening when its cooler."

"Sounds like a plan. We can't stay at mine though. Ciara's stressing about her exams and won't let anyone make any noise past 9 o'clock."

A thought popped into my head.

"Actually, I'll sleep at Danny's which gives you a chance to bring home a hot piece of ass."

"Aww Ruby, constantly my fabulous wing-woman."

He wrapped his arms around me, squeezing me tight.

"Obviously I will be telling my mum that I'm here, but Danny only lives a few streets away."

He rolled his eyes at me.

"Doesn't even need to be said, babe."

We went back to cleaning the house. Taylor's parents weren't due back from their trip until tomorrow but we didn't want to leave the cleaning until last minute. I couldn't wait for the pool, spending all day in the sun, reading my book and not worrying about anymore exams.

Chapter 31
28th May

Today was by far the hottest day of the summer and it was only 9 o'clock. Me and some old friends from college had decided to go to the big outdoor pool to cool off and boy was I glad. We had secured a prime spot under the big oak tree and arrived here early to avoid most of the queues.

"Hey bro, isn't that the girl you've been banging?" Matt elbowed me in the stomach to get my attention.

I looked up and saw Ruby. I let my eyes wander up and down her delicious body. She was wearing cute denim shorts and the bikini top I remember taking off her on her birthday.

I was about to call her over when I noticed her companion. She had her arm linked through the arm of a shirtless boy and the two of them were laughing away. I turned away in rage. How could she do this to me? After I had told her I loved her as well.

Before I could get up and go or hide somewhere until they had passed, Tom called out, "Yo, Ruby."

She glanced about, hearing her name being called. Finding our party, she smiled and started heading over to us. She pulled the boy along with her, saying something which made him smirk.

She approached the blankets, greeting all my friends, having hung out with them several times.

She sat herself down next to me on my blanket and kissed me. Planning to give her the cold shoulder, I couldn't help but kiss her back, enjoying the feel of her lips on mine. We broke apart, hearing a few wolf whistles and claps. Ruby ignored them as always and turned to the boy still standing at the edge of the rug.

"This is Taylor, my best friend."

The boy waved to the group.

"Do you mind if we join you?"

I looked at her, loosing myself in her beautiful blue eyes. I couldn't say no without sounding like a complete jerk. If Ruby said her and the boy were best friends, I would have to take her word for it.

"Of course."

While Taylor spread out their blanket, I kissed her again, wrapping my arm around her waist and pulling her closer, staking my claim on her.

"Get a room, you lovebirds."

I looked up to see Taylor laughing at us and did I imagine it or was there a spark of jealousy in his eyes?

We had a good day at the pool. Well as good as it could go with Ruby's friend hanging around. I kept glaring at Taylor when I thought he or Ruby weren't looking. We swam, sunbathed, ate lots of food and mostly I could forget about the presence of my rival. I had a good distraction though. Every time I felt myself getting riled up, I held Ruby's hand or kissed her full plump lips. And if that didn't work, I just caught a glimpse of her tits. I know typical man response but she is my girlfriend so I feel its justified.

"Hey, Ruby, I'm getting an ice cream, do you want one?" Taylor asked, getting up and fishing around in his trousers for his wallet.

"Of course, I do. Silly question."

I smiled. Ruby always had food on her mind. The smile vanished a few seconds later at Ruby's next words.

"I'll come with you."

Taylor smiled at her and pulled her up. They went off round the corner, laughing and talking, as thick as thieves.

"Oh, damn, Danny. You've got competition there."

Alex slapped me on the shoulder while the rest of my mates chuckled.

"There's no competition. Ruby and Taylor are just friends," I said still staring of in the distance where they had disappeared.

"Yeah, that's why you have a look of thunder on your face," said Tom.

Ignoring my friends, I stood up. Ruby had been gone for ages. Who knows what her and that boy could be doing right now?

"I'm just going to go and check on the queue."

I didn't wait for a reply and headed off to the food stall round the corner.

I stopped dead in my tracks when I saw Ruby and Taylor in the line, a couple of people in front of them. I breathed a sigh of relief. They really were just friends.

I was about to turn away when I heard Ruby's laugh. She had her back to me but I would recognise that laugh anywhere. She grabbed Taylor's arm, reached up and kissed his check in the most loving gesture I've ever seen.

I turned to walk away but not before noticing that Taylor saw me and whispered to Ruby. Her head darted round and our eyes locked. I couldn't take it anymore. I turned away and started walking towards the entrance.

"Danny, wait."

I heard Ruby's foot steps behind me but I kept walking. If I saw her face right now, I would snap.

"Danny."

Her hand came round my arm, pulling my body round to face her. I kept my gaze on her shoulder to avoid her eyes.

"What was that about?"

Her simple question made me see red. She was acting like I was in the wrong when I had just seen her kiss another guy.

"What was that?" I drew my eyes up to her face, anger clouding my vision.

"I came round to see what was taking so long and I see you kissing someone else."

"Danny…"

Before she could start spilling lies, I wrenched my arm out of her grasp and started walking away.

"So, you're not even going to let me explain?"

She kept up with me.

"Taylor is my best friend and we've known each other since we were in nappies."

"Precisely, allowing time for feelings to come out."

"Danny, you have to believe me, I'm not Tay's type."

"Then how come when I kissed you, he looked at me with jealously?"

"Because he's gay, Danny."

I stopped. Ruby had stopped a couple of paces behind me and I turned to look at her.

"He is more into you than me," she said softly. "I thought you knew. He doesn't try to hide it."

I could do nothing but stare at her. She closed the distance between us and cupped her hands around my face.

"It's you I love and it's you I want to be with. But Tay is my best friend in the whole world and I don't know what I would do without him. And I just want my two best boys to get along because you both mean so much to me," she said, her eyes never leaving mine.

I felt my arms draw around her waist.

"Are you sure he's gay?"

Her arms went around my neck, pulling me closer.

"100% gay. And if you spent half the time talking to him as you do staring at my boobs then you would have realised that by now."

I grinned.

"You noticed that then."

Her only response was to kiss me. I responded by pushing my lips on to hers and pulling her so close there was barley an inch between us.

She pulled back.

"Didn't you meet Taylor at our party?"

I shook my head.

"I was a little busy that night entertaining my sexy girlfriend." I kissed her again. "And besides, why didn't you tell me? We've been dating for a couple of months and we were friends before that."

"It's not something you just blurt out. It's not as if I go 'this is gay Taylor'. Just as I don't introduce you as Cute Danny."

"I'm not cute."

She just laughed and pushed herself up to kiss me.

****

Danny was jealous. Of Taylor. I couldn't believe it. Me and Danny walked back to our friends, hand in hand.

"Did you two go off to finally bang?" one of Danny's mates jeered and there were cat calls from the rest of the group.

Before Danny could open his mouth, I said, "Yeah round by the boys' showers."

I turned to Danny.

"Oh, baby, do you think the security camera caught us?"

The boys all stared at me with open mouthed expressions.

"Careful, boys, you don't want to catch any flies."

I sat back down, Danny lying beside me, his head resting on my leg. I winked at Taylor, letting him know that all was well between me and Danny. Taylor rolled his eyes in response.

I glanced down at Danny. While he was talking to his mates, his fingers were gently caressing my thigh, his actions hidden from everyone else. I still couldn't believe he was jealous of Taylor. I ran my hands through his hair, delighting in the soft waves. He turned his head slightly, smiled at me and gently kissed my leg. His eyes sparkled with love and passion.

Chapter 32
16th September

The summer had been so good. I had sunbathed, read countless books, hung out with Taylor and Danny, both together and separately and spent quality time with my mum and sisters.

At the start of September, I had started my new job. I had managed to find a job at my local junior school, working as a teaching assistant. Following Danny's example, I had decided to take a year out before going to university. This way, I could gain valuable classroom experience before training to be a teacher and earn money while I did it.

I smiled as I remembered the day me and Danny both handed in our notices at the supermarket. We had decided to quit our jobs before the start of the summer holidays, allowing us to spend more time together and with friends and family.

The only down side was that Danny was going to university this year so I wouldn't see him as much. We hadn't talked about it much, preferring to live in the moment and not spoil our summer together. I trusted our relationship; we would get through the long-distance thing together and come out stronger than ever. Danny was going to the University of

Wales and even though it was far away, we promised to see each other as much as possible.

Today was the day he was leaving; his mum and dad were driving him to Wales. He had chosen to go on a Saturday, so that we could spend Friday night together and I could see them off the following morning.

Standing on his driveway, I hugged him goodbye one last time, squeezing on tight and transferring all my love with that one hug. Last night, Danny had made love to me, holding me close, caressing every part of my body, leaving no part untouched or unloved.

Pulling apart from each other, I kissed him briefly, wanting to pull him back inside and take it further but knowing he had to get on the road soon as he and his parents had a long drive ahead of them. He got in the car, waving to me and his sister, Stella, who was standing beside me. A few tears escaped my eyes, but I brushed them aside quickly before Danny could see them. I don't know why I was crying; I would be going down to Wales in a few weeks to see Danny for the weekend. The car pulled forward and I stood watching it as it pulled out of sight.

I turned to Stella.

"I'll see you soon."

I gave her a brief hug and turned to go.

"Yeah, see you soon. Don't be a stranger."

I waved as she went back into the house. Over the course of my friendship and then relationship with Danny, me and Stella had developed our own friendship. Not a 'let's braid each other's hair at sleepovers' kind of friends but I could count on her as a mate. I think it was important to be friends with your boyfriend's family and I knew that Danny loved his family more than everything. He had also developed a close bond with my family, my mum especially.

Danny had tried to ask about my dad a few times but I shut him down each time. My father wasn't something I wanted to discuss with anyone, only Taylor knew the full extent of my hatred for my dad. When Ella was born, my dad had decided that actually a family wasn't what he wanted so had upped and left while Mum was still in the hospital. Last I heard of him, he was sleeping around somewhere in America.

But I didn't need a father and Danny had respected me enough to leave it alone. That was one of the many reasons I loved him. Always putting me first.

I rounded my street and seeing my mum's car parked out front, I practically ran the rest of the way. Recently, Mum had been working overtime at the hospital so we rarely ever saw her for more than 10 minutes at a time. Opening the door, I went straight to the living room, wanting to see my lovely mother.

She was sitting on the sofa with her feet up, a cup of tea in one hand and a book in the other. She glanced up when she saw me enter and went back to her book. I sat down beside her, waiting for her to get to a chapter break. There was nothing worse than being interrupted mid-paragraph. Mum put her book mark in between the pages and smiled at me.

"Has Danny left then?"

"Yeah, he's probably on the motorway by now."

She nodded. I made to get up to leave her in peace to read when she caught my arm in her hand.

"Ruby, before you go, I know you have been spending the night at Danny's a lot and I just wanted to make sure you are being safe."

I went red, hanging my head in embarrassment.

"Mum!"

"I just wanted to check, honey. You're still my baby and far too young to have a baby of your own."

I spluttered.

"Don't worry, we are being safe."

She smiled and let go off my arm. I turned around and quickly legged it to my room. My mother knew when I had started having sex, saying that as long as I was careful and having fun, she didn't mind. She had suggested me going on the pill and for a couple of years, I did, only coming off it recently. Still, it was quite embarrassing to hear it again. I'm just glad that she didn't go into the whole sex talk like I got when I was 12.

My phone buzzed in my pocket, distracting me from my mother's words.

I miss you so much. I can't believe I won't see you for a couple of weeks. Xx

I smiled. Danny was so cute.

I miss you too, looking forward to seeing you at the end of the month. xx

Do you know what I'm going to miss the most? xx Danny replied.

What? xx

Hearing you scream my name as I come inside of you xx

I looked up from my phone, flopping down onto my bed. Boy was the next few weeks going to drag.

Chapter 33
20th October

I kept glancing at the clock, wishing time would go faster. Mum was picking me up straight after school and taking me to the train station. My bag was all packed and waiting in the car. I couldn't wait. Today I was finally seeing Danny again after a month apart.

A child called my name and I pulled myself back to the present. I was currently working with a small group of children on extra maths help. I smiled at the child, bending down to help him answer a question. I banished all thought of Danny and Wales and trains from my mind, concentrating on the children in front of me.

Ever since Danny had gone to uni, I had been finding it so hard without him. Going from seeing each other every day to only speaking on the phone, wasn't doing me any favours. Thankfully, we spoke every day and messaged each other constantly. Taylor was also a massive help, coming home some weekends to have movie nights and sleepovers. Taylor had gone to Cambridge University, studying some science shit. To the absolute shock of our entire year at college, he had achieved the highest grades of the year because everyone always takes him for a pretty boy but actually, he is super smart. He had said to me later that it had felt so good to put those basic bitches in their place.

Finally, the class teacher called for silence and asked the children to put away their work and tidy up the classroom. I asked my group to do the same, putting their maths books in a pile ready for me to mark. The children all went to gather their coats and bags from the cloakroom and sat down in their seats, ready for their daily story.

While they listened, I started marking the maths books. The sooner I was finished, the sooner I could leave. Once the class had been dismissed to their parents and I had finished my marking, the teacher, Shelly came over and we discussed work for after half term and the children's progress today.

I loved my job, working with children all day, seeing them sparkle and learn new things. I couldn't wait to start teaching next year.

"Shelly, do you need anything else doing?"

"Thanks, Ruby, but I think we have it sorted. Have a good half term."

"I will. You too."

I grabbed my coat and bag and left the classroom. Leaving the school grounds, I found my mum's car parked out front. I hopped in and she pulled away.

"Hi, Mum."

"Hi, honey, how was your day?"

We chatted about what I had done until the train station came into view. Mum parked and kissed my check.

"Your bag is in the boot. I've added a box of brownies for you and Danny to enjoy."

"Thanks, Mum, you're the best."

"I know. Text me when you are on the train and when Danny meets you at the station. Don't drink too much. Be safe."

"OK. I'll see you in a week. Bye. Love you."

"Love you too."

I waved her off as she drove away and then went to find my train. Luckily, it was leaving in 10 minutes so I had plenty of time to find the correct platform and then find my seat. I stowed my bag in the overhead compartment and settled down into my seat. I pulled my phone out, shooting a text to Mum, Taylor and Danny before putting my head phones in. I reached into my handbag, getting my book out and settled back to enjoy the long train ride with no interruptions.

Once we pulled into the station in Swansea, I got up, pulling my bag along with me. There wasn't a lot of people in my carriage so I let them leave before me, taking the time to mentally prepare myself.

I stepped off the train, my case heavy in my hands. I scanned the platform but didn't see Danny. He must be waiting outside for me. I pulled my phone out, quickly texting my mother before she could worry. I was about to text Danny to say I was here, when my phone pinged.

Look up xx was all Danny's message said.

I looked up, finding Danny right in front of me. I dropped my case, launching myself into his arms. His arms encircled me, while mine came around his neck. We stayed like that, holding on tight for what felt like hours. When we finally pulled away, it was only to smash our lips together. I kissed him like he was my life source, putting everything into the kiss, showing him how much I had missed him.

We only pulled apart when people started banging into us and making noises of disapproval. I grinned sheepishly at Danny, who in turn only had eyes for me. He gave me one more brief kiss and released me. He picked up my bag in one hand and grabbed my hand with the other. We started walking through the station, towards the exit.

"I'm so glad your finally here. I haven't been able to concentrate on lectures all week."

Danny looked down at me, lust and love crowding his eyes.

"I know the feeling. Time seemed to stand still and I felt that I would never leave school."

Danny just squeezed my hand in response. I leant into his arm, enjoying the warmth of him.

"I have to warn you, I've come straight from work."

He glanced down at my dress, peeping out from under my coat.

"Well then, we'll just have to take it off and put you in something more suitable."

His eyes met mine and I could see the desire pooling in them.

"And what kind of clothes do you think I need?"

The hand not holding his stroked down his arms, trailing lightly along his coat, making him shiver as though I was touching bare skin.

"For what I'm thinking, you won't be needing much clothing."

I groaned and our pace picked up, both of us eager to be back at his flat.

"Oh, by the way, Taylor brought you a present."

Danny frowned.

"What did he get me?"

"Well, you can see it when we get to your flat because I'm kinda wearing it."

I smirked at him, fingering the zip at the top of my dress. I loved this dress. It was a suitable length and style for school but it had a zip which I could lower or raise depending on the occasion. While on the train, I had lowered the zip to the furthest point it could go so that my breasts were on full display.

Danny's throat released a low growl.

"God, Ruby. Are you trying to kill me?"

I laughed, pressing my body against his side, knowing he would feel the weight of my breasts.

Danny stopped us and before I could ask why, he pushed me against a lamp post and kissed me, his lips bruising mine in the intensity of the kiss. I responded in kind, reaching up on tiptoes to completely mould our bodies together.

Danny's fingers started reaching under my coat and I pulled myself off his lips.

"Not yet, tiger."

He groaned and pulled me the rest of the way to his flat which thankfully was close by. He unlocked the door and we went inside. Before we could make it down the hall, the kitchen door opened and a blonde-haired boy poked his head out.

"Yo, Danny, I thought I heard you come in. We're playing ring of fire if you want to join." Noticing me he added, "And your gorgeous friend of course."

"Back off, Sam, she's taken."

Sam put his hands up at though surrendering and went back into the kitchen.

"Do you want to play?" Danny asked me.

I pretended to think about it. Normally I loved any kind of drinking games but I had been waiting a month for Danny and I wasn't prepared to wait for a second longer.

Reading my obvious desire in my eyes, Danny said, "I'll introduce you to them all and then I'll give you the guided tour."

His eyes twinkled as he led me into the kitchen.

The kitchen area was small but cosy, with a table and some chairs in the middle.

"Hey guys, this is my girlfriend, Ruby. Ruby these are my flat mates, Sam, Jessica, Toby, Kieran and Annie."

Danny pointed to each person around the table and everyone either waved or said hello.

"Are you both joining us?" A tall brunette girl asked.

"Nah, I'm going to give Ruby the guided tour but maybe later."

We left the kitchen and Danny stopped in front of a door three down from the front door. He pushed it open, dropped my bag on the floor and turned to me. My coat was already on the floor and Danny slid his arms around me, kicking the door closed behind us.

Without wasting even the smallest second, our lips met, exploring, teasing. Our fingers fumbled around buttons and zips until we both stood in our underwear. My eyes raked down Danny's chest and stomach, coming to rest on his erection, poking proudly out through his boxers. At the same time, I felt his eyes on me, taking in Taylor's 'present', his eyes lighting up with desire.

"Well, you can tell Taylor that I love the present but I prefer what's underneath."

He kissed a trail of butterfly kisses along my jaw and down my neck. I arched my body, silently begging for his attention. He kept kissing, reaching my breasts, pushing them up and over the top of the silk teddy. His fingers trailed a path down my body, his lips still peppering my neck with kisses. I felt him move my pants aside, brushing his fingers against me. Without warning, he thrust his finger inside me, his thumb stroking my clit.

"Danny..." I panted, clinging on to his shoulders for support.

He withdrew his finger and before I could protest, he slipped two in. He thrust his fingers in and out, setting a harsh rhythm. I could feel my orgasm building up, threatening to take over my entire body.

I pulled Danny's head back to mine, I needed him now, I couldn't wait another moment. I pushed him back towards the bed, taking of my bra as I went. Danny's boxers came off just as he fell on to the bed, grabbing my waist and pulling me on top of his hard body. I straddled his hip, feeling his hard length pushing against me. I shimmied out of my pants and slid myself onto Danny, letting out a sigh of contentment as he filled me.

Danny grabbed my hips, letting me set a fast-paced rhythm as our hips bucked in time with each other. I threw my head back, feeling Danny fill me even more as I rode him until we both came, me falling limp on top of his chest and Danny wrapping his arms round me.

I released Danny from between my legs and I flopped down on the bed next to him. We both took a minute to catch our breaths. Danny turned to me, placing a light kiss by my eyebrow. His arms squeezed me tight as my fingers danced lightly over his chest.

"I have missed this," he said.

I chuckled.

"What? The sex?"

"Yeah, that's all I missed."

Danny smirked.

I slapped Danny's arm lightly but he caught my hand and kissed it gently, his actions betraying his words.

"I have also missed seeing your gorgeous face and holding you in my arms."

I propped myself up on his chest, kissing him briefly.

"I know, it's been far too long but it has been hectic at work and home."

His fingers trailed lazily up and down my arm, coming to rest at my fingers which he picked up and held tight in his.

"Uni has been full-on as well. We've had non-stop lectures and essays to do. But I'm glad you're here now."

"Same."

I kissed him, dragging my body up his to reach his lips. He responded, kissing me tenderly.

I pulled away, smiling down at him.

"Do you want to go and show your flat mates how much I can drink them under the table?"

He grinned.

"Nothing would make me happier."

Danny rolled out of bed and pulled on his boxers. He chucked me my underwear and one of his t-shirts. I pulled them on and found my jeans and the bottle of vodka in my bag. I turned around, finding Danny dressed and holding the door open for me. I took his hand and we made our way back to the kitchen.

Entering the kitchen, Danny pulled out a chair and sat down. Seeing no other chairs, I sat on his lap, placing the vodka on the table.

"Hey, guys, we thought we would join now."

Sam, the blond from before, passed me a glass and I poured a few shots into it. Seeing the shocked look on their faces, I just smirked.

"Well, I've got some catching up to do, haven't I?"

I poured vodka in Danny's glass and topped them both of with lemonade.

"Well, newcomer, pick a card."

I laughed, reaching forward to pick up a card from the ring in the middle.

"Six, dicks drink up."

The guys lifted their cups and clinked them in the middle, before taking huge mouthfuls.

We played until everyone was very tipsy, moving on to 'never have I ever' and general chat. I stayed on Danny's lap for the whole time, one of his arms a permanent feature round my waist.

I don't know if it was the alcohol or not but I swear I could see Annie, the tall brunette making eyes at Danny across the table. I couldn't see if he was looking at her due to me sitting on his lap but every time I glanced across the table, I could see her. One time she caught me looking and glared at me. I simply leant back into Danny's chest, turning my head to plant a quick but loving kiss on his lips. If possible, Annie's eyes gained even more heat and if looks could kill, I would be a pile of ash on the floor.

I trusted Danny completely but her not so much. Without it ruining my week, I vowed to keep an eye on her, making my claim on Danny very clear.

Chapter 34
21st October

I woke up to a warmth behind me, a weight over my stomach and Danny's familiar scent drifting over my senses. I smiled. This was the way I wanted to wake up for the rest of my life.

I turned my body slightly, not wanting to wake Danny up. I lightly pushed some of his hair out of his eyes, my fingers trailing down his cheek. I felt his arm pull me tighter to him, making our bodies flush against each other.

"I didn't mean to wake you," I whispered.

"You didn't. I've been awake for a few minutes. I like staring at you while you sleep."

"Wow that's not creepy at all."

Danny's only response was to kiss me, his lips lingering on mine in a soft embrace.

"Morning, beautiful."

"Morning, handsome." I smiled at him. "I could stay like this forever," I said, resting my head on Danny's chest.

"I'll just have to chain you here to be my sex slave until the end of time."

Danny chuckled. While he spoke, his fingers had started running down my stomach, across my legs and under the shirt I was wearing.

I nestled my body closer to his, liking what his fingers were doing to me.

"And what will I tell the school? Or my mother?" I asked, my own fingers trailing down his bare chest to his boxers.

"I think that's something we can deal with later. Right now, I've got a rather large problem that needs your immediate attention."

He glanced down briefly at his erection.

"Thinking very highly of yourself, are we? Though I suppose I can help you out."

Kissing him, I pushed his boxers down and he kicked them fully off. I felt his hands under my shirt as he pushed it up and over my body. Danny rolled over me, pushing me into the mattress.

Sometime later, after sharing a shower and dressing between kisses, we made it out into the bright October day. We strolled along the path, our hands linked and swinging between us. We chatted as we walked, Danny talking about uni and me telling him about my job and the school.

We had plans for the week, but honestly, I hadn't listened when Danny told me what we were doing. I was just happy to be finally holding his hand, being close to him after several weeks apart. This week was going to fly by and I intended to grab every moment I could with Danny.

Over the week, we hung out with his flat mates, we ventured into several clubs and spent a lot of time just being in each other's presence. It was a blissful week. By the end, I was seriously considering taking up Danny's offer of being chained to his bed and staying with him forever.

As I was gathering my clothes strewn over the floor, Danny was lounging on his bed, his eyes following my movements.

"That's mine."

He pointed to a shirt I was currently folding into my bag.

I ignored him, putting the shirt in my bag anyway.

"Can you pass that skirt?"

Danny pulled the skirt out from under his leg where I had thrown it last night in a drunken haze.

"Not until I get my shirt back."

"That's where you're wrong. This shirt came with me into Wales and will leave with me from Wales."

"Well then, I'm keeping the skirt."

"I don't think it's your colour," I said, pretending to think it over. "Besides, what would your flat mates think?"

"They will obviously think that I am very sexy and won't be able to keep their eyes off me."

He smirked and held my skirt up against his hips.

I went over and took the skirt out of his hands and threw it in the general direction of my bag.

"I see your aim hasn't improved in the slightest."

"It's nearly in the bag. I just have more pressing matters right in front of me."

I sat down beside Danny, resting my arms and head on his stomach and looking up at his face.

"Can I keep the shirt?"

I batted my eyelids at him and pouted slightly.

Danny just kept his gaze locked with mine, his arms behind his head.

"I suppose you can. But there will have to be some form of payment involved."

I could feel his chest rumbling as he spoke and I climbed over his body to straddle him.

"And what kind of payment are you thinking of, sir?"

I wiggled my hips slightly, feeling Danny's erection harden beneath me.

"I'm sure I can think of something."

And with that he pulled me down, claiming my lips in a fierce loving kiss.

Chapter 35
3rd November

Walking back from work, I let myself into the house, finding it empty. Both my sisters were still at school and Mum was at work. I loved these days the best, having the whole house to myself, especially after a long day at work. I grabbed an apple from the kitchen and started walking upstairs, my fingers automatically pressing Danny's name on my contacts to facetime him.

Today had been my second observation from my tutor who came into school every month or so to observe me with a small group or the class, teaching something that I had planned. I had been so nervous that I couldn't sleep last night but now it was over and my tutor had given me a good review. I couldn't wait to tell Danny how it had gone.

The call connected and it took me a moment to realise that the person who answered wasn't Danny.

"Hi."

I just stared at the screen. Filling my phone was Annie, sitting on Danny's bed and I could see her lacy bra strap at the edge of the screen, hanging off her bare shoulder.

"Can I help you?" Annie asked, sounding bored and inspecting her nails.

"Where's Danny?"

"In the shower."

She smirked.

"You very nearly missed us; I was just about to jump in with him."

I opened my mouth to speak, to ask her if she was joking, to say Danny would never do something like this, to say anything really when she went on before my brain could process what she was saying.

"Well, I really do need a shower, especially after the hot and kinky sex I've just had with your boyfriend. I'll be sure to tell Danny that you called though."

And with that, the screen went black as she ended the call, leaving me to stare blankly at my phone.

I should call him back to see if this was just some huge practical joke but my fingers wouldn't move. No, I thought to myself. I wouldn't call him. I had seen, with my own eyes, Annie in her skimpy clothes and I could hear the shower running over her snide remarks. I had thought that he was better than this, that what we had was real. But as soon as he could, he was straight into bed with someone else and who knows how long he had been sleeping around and with who knows how many girls.

I threw my phone across the bed and curled up in a ball under my duvet, where I stayed until my mum came home and found me.

A couple of days later, I had dragged myself home and silenced my phone for the 100th time. It was Danny ringing. Again. Ever since I had found out that he had cheated on me, I had been ignoring his calls and texts. Danny had been persistent trying every day to reach me, waking me up in the mornings and not stopping until late at night.

Opening the front door, I angrily jabbed my finger on the answer call button. I couldn't take this anymore. I had to speak to him and end it because I couldn't live with the pain.

"Go away, Danny. I don't want to speak to you."

"Ruby! Why? What's wrong?"

"Don't act as though you don't know, you filthy, lying shithead."

"Ruby, I haven't got a clue what you are talking about."

It annoyed me further that he was so calm about everything especially considering he knew how I felt about cheating as my dad had cheated on my mum several times.

"You are a cheating scumbag. Danny, we are over. I can't bear to look at you anymore. You can go back to screwing Annie and whoever else takes your fancy but we are done. Don't call me again."

And with that, I hung up. My phone immediately rang again but I ended the call and before Danny could ring again, I blocked his number. I slid down the wall, still in my coat and shoes, bag still in hand. I sat on the floor and cried. Great big sobs that wracked my entire body. I pressed my face into my knees, not caring about my mascara which was surely running down my face by now.

Reaching for my phone, I rang Taylor who I knew didn't have any lectures on today. He picked up on the first ring and before I could get a single word out, I burst into tears again.

When I had no more tears left to cry, I told Taylor the whole story of how another woman had answered Danny's phone, her admitting that they had sex and me breaking up with Danny.

"Tay, can I come and stay with you this weekend? I just need my best friend."

"Sure, honey. We can watch movies and get drunk and eat for England."

"Thanks, Tay, I really do not know what I would do without you. I'll see you on Friday."

I ended the call and went to pack my overnight bag ready for tomorrow. I sighed. Only one more day to get through before seeing my best friend who would make the world right again for me.

Chapter 36
Present Day

The four of us were sitting in the living room of our flat, trying to work but really, we were just talking. In hindsight, we actually did better work at the library or in our own separate rooms but sometimes we liked to sit together and pretend to work and occasionally bouncing ideas of each other.

"Just out of curiosity…" Jo trailed off, still looking at her computer screen but her attention on me.

"What happened with you and Danny?" said Gina.

"Please tell us."

Emily joined the conversation.

I sighed, marking my place in the text book I was trying to read.

"Things between me and Danny were going great. Amazing, even. Everyone thought we would stay together for years if not more. My best friend, Taylor had even started writing his maid of honour speech."

"So, what went tits up?" Jo probed.

"I went to visit him in Wales, after a few months of not seeing each other. The saying, 'absence makes the heart grow fonder' is true, we had explosive sex, I spent time with all of his flat mates and we spent time together. It was one of the best weeks of my life. And then a few weeks later, I ring him to tell him about my recent observation at work and another woman answers the call. To make it worse, it was one of his flat mates who when I visited, had been making eyes at Danny while I was right there."

Jo, Gina and Emily all stared at me with a mixture of love for me and hatred for Danny in their eyes. Emily held onto my hand for morale support and squeezed tight. I squeezed her hand back; glad I was surrounded by friends.

"Annie, the slut on the phone, said that she and Danny had just had sex and were about to go for round two in the shower. And then she hung up. Danny kept calling and calling me but I ignored him until I eventually answered. I yelled at him, broke up with him and then blocked his number."

"And you hadn't heard from him until recently?" Emily asked.

"But more importantly, why is he here all of a sudden?" Gina added.

"And are you going to see him again now he is back?" Jo leaned forward so that I now had all three pairs of eyes staring at me.

Honestly, I didn't know what I was going to do. Sleeping with Danny again was a mistake and a lapse in judgement. I quite clearly still loved him if I was ready to jump into bed with him the minute he shows up with a soft smile and kind eyes. But was I ready to forgive him for cheating on me and then not seeing him for a year?

I was about to start putting my disordered thoughts into words for my friends when the doorbell rang. I sighed with relief. Saved by the bell.

"I'll go. I think it's my amazon delivery anyway."

I ran down the hall way, wanting to catch the delivery guy before he decided that no one was home and left, taking my package with him.

I opened the door. "Tha…" My hand stopped mid reach when I saw that it wasn't the postman or the amazon delivery guy but was in fact Danny.

"What are you doing here?"

I kept my hand on the door handle, ready to slam the door in his cheating face.

"Just because I let my emotions get the better of me the other night and we slept together, does not mean that you are welcome here."

Just as I was about to push the door closed on him, his foot slid over the threshold, blocking my attempts at slamming the door.

"Ruby, I just want to speak to you."

"Go away, Danny. Go back to fucking your bimbos and not making my life hell."

His foot fell away from the door, a hurt look crossing his features.

"I guess if that's how you feel, then I'll go."

He turned away and started walking down the road while I stood and watched him leave.

I shut the door, only when he was out of sight and trudged back to the living room. No one said a word as I picked up my laptop and glared at the screen furiously. Emily rested her head against my shoulder but no one said anything, which I was grateful for. Later I would talk about it but I couldn't get the words out right now.

"Hey, Ruby, what time did you say Taylor was coming up?"

"Um, he said that he was getting the 3 o'clock train so he should be here any time soon."

Taylor had been coming to see me regularly and had inserted himself with my uni friends as seamlessly as if he knew them from birth. It was one of the things I loved about him, that when he wanted to, he could be friends with just about anybody. He was coming to visit this weekend and the 5 of us were going out clubbing and Taylor couldn't get here soon enough. I needed the alcohol to drown my sorrows and forget that I ever met Danny.

Chapter 37

When we heard another knock at the door, I refused to open it, instead letting Gina go and answer the door. Hearing squeals, I knew who was at the door, my thoughts confirmed when my best friend walked through the door.

"Hey, bitchesss. The life of the party has arrived so shut down those laptops and get the vodka out."

I jumped up and threw my arms round his neck, his arms squeezing my waist in return. I released him, letting him hug everyone else.

He flopped down into the arm chair.

"So, tell me, what's new?"

We all exchanged nervous glances, none of sure whether or not to tell Taylor about Danny showing up at the house again.

"Danny came by today."

I couldn't hide anything from Taylor, he was my best friend who had been by my side through the thick and the thin. He would know the right thing to do. Having already told him about Danny and I sleeping together a few nights ago, I told Taylor about Danny turning up outside my lecture and then again at the house, and what he said each time.

"Well, that bitch. We definitely need to go drinking then. Maybe catch you some rebound guy to shag your feelings away."

"No, tonight I just want to dance the night away with my best girls. No boys."

"Hear, hear sister!"

Jo whooped in the corner.

"I'll pour some drinks and while Em orders the Chinese."

"Ladies I believe this might help our night."

Taylor lifted a giant bottle of vodka out of his bag to the sound of cheers.

That night, we all got so plastered, I don't think I could tell you, my name. Gina managed to get with a guy who swiftly took her back to his place and Taylor scored a few numbers of really cute guys. Why do all the hot ones have to be gay or undatable?

We received a quick drunken message from Gina, letting us know where she was and not to expect her until the morning and continued to dance the night away, only stopping when the lights flooded on and security kicked us out.

The 4 of us went back to our house, still pretty drunk so decided to walk it, hoping that the crisp morning air would help to sober us up. Which it did and I was just left with an empty stomach and a knot of emotions I was in no capable position to start unravelling.

Just as we reached the house and Emily unlocked the door, Jo heading towards the kitchen to start on our post-drinking bacon sandwiches. Taylor caught my arm, pulling me to a stop just inside the doorway.

"I think you should speak to Danny."

I was speechless. I had no words.

"Um, I'm sorry, WHAT?"

"He rang me just as I arrived in Nottingham and at first, I didn't pick up due to the amount of pain he caused you but after the 6th call, I answered. Honey, don't be mad but he explained in part what had happened and I think you need to hear it from him before you make any rash decisions."

I had so many questions but I couldn't voice any of them. My mouth just hung open not listening to my brain.

"Darling, you might want to shut that otherwise you'll be catching flies."

"Tay, why didn't you say anything before?"

"Well, I wanted you to have a night of enjoyment and a night where you could try and forget him but the look in your eyes as we left the club told me everything I needed to know. You still love him, Ruby, and you won't be able to get past this until you hear him out."

I nodded. I knew Taylor was right but I couldn't admit that unless I wanted his head to get even bigger.

"I'm going to go and shower and think over what you've just dropped on me."

Taylor nodded and went into the kitchen to devour a mountain of bacon.

After a long hot shower and a change of clothes, I made my way to the kitchen, hoping to find some bacon left over when the doorbell rang.

"Don't worry, I've got it."

I opened the door and like yesterday, Danny was standing outside, hands stuffed in his coat pockets.

"Before you slam the door in my face again, I just want you to have this."

He handed me a small keyring and walked away without another word.

I opened my palm and gasped in surprise as memories jostled for space in my mind. Danny and me laughing at the beach, us playing in the arcade centre, me winning the keyring on one of those penny drop games and presenting my prize to Danny. I hadn't realised that he had kept it. I clasped it in my hand.

"Wait, Danny."

He stopped and turned my way, an expectant look on his face.

"Why did you keep this?"

He strode towards me, coming close enough that I could almost hear the pounding of his heart.

"I kept it because it reminded me of you and the love, I felt for you."

"If you loved me, you wouldn't have done what you did."

"Ruby, can I come inside, I don't want all your neighbours thinking I'm a complete ass."

"Fine."

I held open the door, letting Danny enter before me.

"In here," I said pointing to the living room.

I could still hear voices from the kitchen and the shower running so I knew we would be OK in here for now. And there was no way we were going back to my bedroom. We wouldn't get *any* talking done there.

Before Danny could start talking, I launched into my attack.

"Where have you been for the last year? Why…"

I got no further before Danny interrupted.

"I need to explain. And I need you to listen. I'll gladly go after you have heard me out if that's what you want."

"OK."

I melted down onto the sofa and Danny took a seat next to me while still giving me space.

"I didn't sleep with her."

"Oh wow, is that it?"

I crossed my arms over my chest.

"Ruby."

He took my hand and just held it between both of his.

"I didn't sleep with her. Annie came into my room while I was in the shower and she must have picked up my phone then. When I came out it was to see her lounging on my bed. She propositioned me but I told her to leave because I had a girlfriend who I loved so much. I would never do anything to hurt you. I didn't even realise that you had called until later on that day at which point, you were ignoring me."

"With good reason."

I huffed, pulling my hand out of his grip but missing the contact immediately.

"But, Danny, I saw the looks she was giving you when I visited. I got scared because I thought that she would take you away from me and then I saw my fears come alive when she answered your phone."

"I'm telling you now that nothing ever happened with her. Or any other girl since you broke up with me. I tried. I wanted to forget about you if you wanted nothing to do with me. I tried sleeping around but I always left before I could do more than kiss someone else."

"Wh... w."

Tears were falling down my face at this point but I couldn't wipe them away.

"For goodness' sake, Ruby, I didn't sleep with Annie."

He thundered into my stunned face.

"Well then why did you take so long to talk to me and tell me what happened? It's been a year, Danny, since we broke up, a year with nothing."

Danny rubbed a hand over his face, looking tired and depressed.

"Taylor rang me after you blocked my number and asked me not to bother you again. To not cause you anymore pain. I agreed but only because I didn't want to be the reason for your tears anymore."

He took both my hands this time and held on as though I was his lifeline.

"But then I saw you in the library and all my old feelings came rushing back. When you agreed to go out to dinner with me, I've never felt happier. I was going to tell you everything there and then but I couldn't find the words and I didn't want to ruin our first night together after so long apart. Yesterday, I rang Taylor and told him that I was going to ignore what he asked me to do and I was going to do everything in my power to get you back."

"Ruby, after that night I realised that I love you. That I still love you. My feelings never went away, they were just buried under grief and hurt."

"How can you say that? You can't come in here after a year saying that you still love me. Danny, I've had feelings for you since we first met, all that time ago on my first shift, stacking groceries."

Danny lent forward at that moment and our lips met in a long, sweet kiss.

"I've been in love with you since I first laid eyes on you, when you walked into the store room and I've loved you every moment since then and I'll continue to love you even if you stop loving me."

His hands cupped my face, his eyes locking with mine. "Tell me to leave and I will but just know that I love you so much and that this last year has been torture for me. Not holding you in my arms, not hearing your voice before I fall asleep and not seeing weird and funny texts from you at odd times in the morning."

I couldn't say anything. Danny still loved me. He hadn't slept with Annie. I was about to open my mouth when Danny sighed and removed his hands from my face.

"I think that's my answer. I'll go now."

He started getting up but my hand shot out of its own accord and held onto his arm.

"Danny…"

Something in my voice must have given me away because he kissed me again, our lips moulding together. We broke apart and I threw my arms around his neck, pulling him towards me, leaving no space between us. Danny's arms came around my waist and I felt his head rest against my shoulder.

"Danny, I love you. I'm so sorry that I didn't let you explain sooner. I've been miserable without you."

Danny brushed his thumbs over my checks, wiping away my tears.

"I love you too. I'm never going to let you go."

With that, our lips fused together, hands exploring body parts as though we were starved people presented with a banquet. I climbed on to his lap, our mouths never breaking apart.

The sound of slow clapping broke us apart and I looked up to see Taylor, Emily, Gina and Jo standing at the living room door.

"What a show. Boy, I'm starting to get hot and bothered just looking at you. Might have to call one of those guys from last night."

Taylor smirked at me, coming to flop down on the sofa.

I slid of Danny's lap, looking sheepishly at my lap.

"Danny, this is Jo, Gina and Emily, my closest friends, without whom, I wouldn't have gotten through this much of uni. Guys, Danny, my um…"

"Her boyfriend." Danny finished for me, sliding his hand over my leg and stroking my knee with his thumb.

"Finally," Jo said, sitting down next to me. "Ever since you slept together last week, we've been routing for you."

"Nearly put money on how long it would take for both of you to come to your senses and get together," Emily added.

"Taylor, do you want to sleep in my room tonight?" Gina asked, raising her eyebrow in the most obvious way she could think of.

I laughed.

"As long as you don't mind that fact that he snores."

"I've had worse bed mates. And at least this one won't try and leave half way through the night or fall asleep mid-way through sex."

I turned to Danny.

"Can you stay? Please."

"Like I said before, I'm never leaving."

****

Pulling on my pyjamas later on that evening, Danny walked back into my room from having a shower.

"What would you say if I finished my degree somewhere a bit closer to home than Wales? Somewhere like Nottingham?"

I glanced at Danny.

"What?"

"Well, the long-distance thing didn't really work out all too well for us so I thought that maybe…"

"You want to finish your degree here?"

"Ruby, I want to finish my degree wherever you are. That's why I came here in the first place. Stella also wanted to look around so we combined our visits. I was going to try and convince you that we need to be together, that I can't live without you. As I told Taylor, I'm stopping at nothing until you are mine again."

"But I can't make you move here just to be with me. We could find somewhere in the middle of us."

"You like it here, you have friends here and besides, next year for me is short and mainly exam based."

He took my hands.

"I just want to be with you."

"Same, I can't imagine a life without you."

I grinned and kissed him.

"Shall we go to bed then?"

His reply was to kiss me, taking my breath away and tumbling us into the covers.

Epilogue
4 Years Later

I woke up to the sun streaming through the blinds. I reached across the bed, expecting to find the warm, sculptured chest of my husband but my arm met nothing but the bedsheets, his side of the duvet pushed back. Opening my eyes, I looked around the room, hoping to see him there but instead, I saw an empty room. I was about to get up to go searching for coffee and breakfast to fully wake myself up when I heard the pattering of feet in the hall outside my room. I smiled to myself, recognising my husband's footsteps and laid back against the pillows.

"Look who's awake now, Georgie," Danny whispered as he pushed open the door.

He walked in carrying our three-year-old daughter in his arms. Georgia was a mini-Danny, looking just like him with clear blue eyes and a tuft of dirty blond hair. Danny put her down on the bed and Georgia climbed over to my waiting arms.

"Hello, my gorgeous girl," I said, cradling my daughter in my arms and pressing my lips to her head. She smiled and then nestled against my body, content to just lying there.

Turning to Danny, I kissed him and said, "I hope you didn't wake her up."

"Would I ever?" he said, his mouth crinkling in effort to stop smiling.

"She was up and standing on her bed and you know that I can't resist those puppy dog eyes."

He pulled a funny face at Georgia, making her gurgle and giggle with delight.

I smiled back at him and kissed him with all the love I felt. He put his arms around me and Georgia and together we lay back on the bed.

Just before I had graduated, I had discovered I was pregnant. I had delayed telling Danny, fearing it would scare him off as we both wanted kids but not right away. However, when I told him, he had thrown his arms around me, sweeping me off my feet and proposing on the spot.

"You're not marrying me because you knocked me up, are you?" I asked.

"Yes, but also no. I've been planning on asking you for a while now. This just sped up the process."

And ever since then, Danny has been smitten with our daughter. Of course, she uses this to her full advantage and has him wrapped round her little finger. But I wouldn't change that for anything.

Besides, in about five months, Georgia will have a little brother or sister, much to both her and her father's delight.

I turned and kissed Danny's chest and he in return kissed my forehead. *No*, I thought, *I wouldn't change anything about my family for anything in the world.*